No one writes romantic fiction like Barbara Cartland.

Miss Cartland was originally inspired by the best of the romantic novelists she read as a girl—Elinor Glyn, Ethel Dell, Ian Hay and E. M. Hull. Convinced that her own wide audience would also delight in her favorite authors, Barbara Cartland has taken their classic tales of romance and specially adapted them for today's readers.

Bantam is proud to publish these novels—personally selected and edited by Miss Cartland —under the imprint

BARBARA CARTLAND'S
LIBRARY OF LOVE

Bantam Books by Barbara Cartland
Ask your bookseller for the books you have missed

Barbara Cartland's Library of Love

HIS HOUR
BY ELINOR GLYN
CONDENSED BY
BARBARA CARTLAND

BANTAM BOOKS · TORONTO · NEW YORK · LONDON

HIS HOUR
A Bantam Book / March 1977

ISBN 0–553–10498–5

Published simultaneously in the United States and Canada

Bantam Books are published by Bantam Books, Inc. Its trade-
mark, consisting of the words "Bantam Books" and the por-
trayal of a bantam, is registered in the United States Patent
Office and in other countries. Marca Registrada, Bantam
Books, Inc., 666 Fifth Avenue, New York, New York 10019.

PRINTED IN THE UNITED STATES OF AMERICA

Preface
by
Barbara Cartland

When I was young Elinor Glyn was spoken of
with bated breath. Her books were considered ex-
termely improper and not *"pour les jeune filles."*
But I always loved *His Hour* because Russia
fascinated me as it fascinated Elinor. She was
asked by the Grand Duchess Kiril of Russia in
the summer of 1909 to spend the winter in St.
Petersburg with a view to writing a book about
the Russian Court.

She arrived in December and for the next
two months was entertained royally. She was
shown round the Winter Palace by two Grand
Dukes and lesser Royalty. Without having been
there she seemed to know her way and she explained to the staid Grand Duke Andre that
she was the re-incarnation of Catherine the Great,
adding for corroboration some details about
Catherine's death which were not at that time
supposed to be known in Russia.

She made notes for a novel, worked out
scenes incorporating a Prince who had recently

been killed in a duel. Her own adventures in Russia were frighteningly exciting and at the same time quite incredible, but after she had written the book she returned in May. She read it aloud to the assembled Court in her beautiful low clear speaking voice, of which she was proud.

They were thrilled by her masterful, tempestuous, passionate, and untamable hero, and the romance of Gritzko and Tamara against the splendours of Imperial Russia, the pomp and ceremony, the balls and banquets, the sleigh bells and the snow, will, I know, thrill you.

Chapter
One

The Sphinx was smiling its eternal smile.

It was two o'clock in the morning, and only an Arab or two lingered near the boy who held Tamara's camel, so, but for Hafis, she was alone with her thoughts and the Sphinx.

The blue of the sky seemed to speak of hope. Could any other country produce a sky of so deep a sapphire as the night sky of Egypt?

All round was intense sensuous warmth and stillness almost as light as day.

How wise she had been to break through the conventionality which surrounded her to come here alone, on this one of her last nights in Egypt.

She half smiled when she thought of Millicent Hardcastle's face when she had first suggested it.

"My dear Tamara, what an extraordinary thing for a woman to do! Go to the Sphinx all alone at two o'clock in the morning! Would not people think it very strange?"

"Perhaps, but do you know, Millicent, I don't

1

care. That carven block of stone has had a curious effect upon me. It has made me think as I have never done before."

Even Mrs Hardcastle's mild assertion that it could equally well be studied at a more reasonable hour did not move Tamara.

While her friend slumbered comfortably in her bed at Mena House, she had set off, a self-conscious feeling of being a truant schoolboy exalting her.

Tamara was a widow. James Loraine had been everything that a thoroughly respectable English husband ought to be.

He had treated her with kindness, he had given her a comfortable home, and he had never caused her a moment's jealousy.

She could not remember her heart having beaten an atom faster, or slower, for his coming or going.

She had loved him, and her sisters and brother, and father, all in the same devoted way. When pneumonia had carried him off nearly two years before, she had grieved with the measure that the loss of any one of them would have caused her.

They were such a nice family, Tamara's!

For hundreds of years they had lived on the same land, doing their duty.

They had been Members of Parliament, Generals, riders to hounds, subscribers to charities, rigid Church-goers, and disciplined, orthodox, worthy members of society.

Underdown was their name, and Underwood their home.

That Tamara should have been given that

Russian appellation, in a group of Gladyses, Mabels, and Dorothys, must have surely indicated that fate meant her to follow a line not quite so mapped out as that of her sisters.

The very manner of her entry into the world was not in accordance with the Underdown plan.

Her mother, Lady Gertrude Underdown, had contracted a friendship with the wife of the First Secretary of the Russian Embassy.

The Squire had grumbled, but agreed, when a fourth daughter was presented to him with a request that she should have Princess Vera for a godmother, and a Russian name.

"Foreign fandangoes," he designated such ideas. However, Lady Gertrude was very ill, and had to be humoured, so the baby was christened Tamara.

There were no more Russian suggestions in the family; the son and heir who arrived a year later became plain Tom, and then Lady Gertrude Underdown made her bow to the world and retired to the family vault in Underwood Church.

They were all brought up by an aunt, and hardly ever left the country until each one came up in turn to be presented at Court, and go through a fairly dull Season with their country neighbours.

Two of the daughters, including Tamara, had secured suitable husbands, and at the age of twenty-three years the latter had been left a well-dowered widow.

She had worn mourning for just the right period, had looked after her affairs, and handed James's place over with a good grace to his brother.

3

Two years after her loss, she had allowed herself to be persuaded into taking a trip to Egypt with her friend Millicent Hardcastle, who was recovering from influenza.

Everything had been a kind of shock to her. And driving at night the heavy scent and intoxicating atmosphere had made her blood tingle. She felt it was almost wrong that things should appeal so ardently to her senses.

Without a word of warning a young man rose from a bank of sand where he had been stretched motionless and unperceived.

"A fine goddess, is she not, Madame?" he asked.

To add to the impertinence of a stranger's addressing her, Tamara was further incensed by the voice being that of a foreigner.

But it was an extraordinarily pleasant voice, deep and tuneful, and the insolent stranger stood over six feet high, and in spite of his square shoulders and air of strength was as slender as Tamara herself.

She hardly knew what to answer, he had spoken with such ease and assurance, almost with the tone of one who hails a fellow worshipper and has a right to exchange sympathy.

Tamara had been startled when she thought she was alone, but at last she answered slowly:

"Yes."

"I often come here at night," he went on, "then you get her alone, and she says things to you. You think so, too, don't you?"

"Yes," said Tamara again, astonished at herself for speaking at all.

"At first I was angry when I saw your camel

4

against the sky, and saw you dismount to sit and look. I like to have her all to myself. But afterwards when I watched you I saw you meant no harm, you aren't a tourist, and so you did not matter!"

"Indeed," Tamara remarked.

"Yes," he continued, unconcerned. "You can't look at that face and feel we any of us matter much. Can you?"

"No."

"How many thousand years has she been telling people that? But it drives me mad, angry, furious, to see the tourists! I want to strangle them all!"

He clenched his hands and his eyes flashed.

Tamara peeped at him. He was not looking at her, but at the Sphinx. She saw that he was extremely attractive in spite of looking un-English.

The Underdown part of her questioned if he could be quite a gentleman.

But when he turned his face full upon her in the moonlight, that doubt vanished completely. He might even be a very great gentleman, she thought.

"Would you like to see a bit of the Arabian Nights?" he asked her.

Tamara rose. This really ought not to go on, this conversation, and yet . . .

"Yes, I would," she said.

"Let us go together and see something else that is very interesting."

"What?" asked Tamara.

"The Sheikh's village down below. Half the people who come don't realise it is there, and the

5

other half would be afraid to ride through it at night. But they know me and I will take care of you."

Without the least further hesitation he called Hafis and the camel, spoke to them in Arabic, and then stood ready to help Tamara into the saddle.

She seemed hypnotised. She began to realise that she was going into the unknown with a perfect stranger, but she did not think of turning back.

"What do you ride?" she asked.

"See!" he exclaimed, and gave a strange low whistle, which was instantly answered by the equally strange low whinny of a horse.

From the foot of the rocks a beautiful Arabian horse appeared.

"I am taking him back with me," he said. "Isn't he a beauty? I only bought him a week ago, and already he knows me."

Then he was in the saddle with the lightest bound, and Tamara, who had always admired Tom on a horse, knew that she had never seen anyone who seemed so much a part of his mount as this quaint foreigner.

"I suppose he is an Austrian," she said to herself, and then added with English insular arrogance, "Only Austrians are like us."

The young man appeared quite indifferent to anything she thought. He started to lead the way down beyond the Sphinx, apparently into the desert.

Now that he was in front of her, Tamara could not help admiring the lines of his figure. He was certainly a very elegant shape, and certainly knew how to ride.

The young man rode in front until they were on the flat desert, then drew rein and waited for her.

"You see," he said, "we skirt these rocks and then we shall ride through the village. One can very well imagine it has always been the same."

They entered the little town. The streets were extremely narrow and the dark houses had an air of mystery.

There was a deep silence and the moonlight made the shadows sharp as a knife.

A shaft of red light would shoot from some strange low hovel as they passed, and they could see inside a circle of Bedouin Arabs crouching over a fire. Their faces were solemn as the grave.

Presently, in the narrowest and darkest street, there was a sound of tom-toms, strains of weird music, and voices.

Through the chinks of the half-open shutters, light streamed across the road, while a small crowd of Arabs was grouped about the gate in the wall holding donkeys and a camel.

"A wedding," said the young man. "They have escorted the bride."

Tamara looked up at the window. She wondered what could be happening within; were the other wives there as well? She would have liked to ask.

The young man saw her hesitation and said laconically:

"Well?"

7

"They are having a party?" Tamara questioned.

"Of course," said the young man. "Weddings and funerals are equally good occasions for company. They are so wise they leave all to fate; they do not tear their eyes out for something they cannot have. They are philosophers, these Arabs."

The little crowd round the gate now barred the road, half good-humoredly, half with menace.

"So, so," said the young man, riding in front.

He laughed, and putting his hand in his pocket brought out a quantity of silver and flung it among them with merry words in Arabic, while he pointed to the windows of the house.

Then he seized the bridle of Tamara's camel and started his horse forward. The crowd smiled now and began scrambling for the baksheesh, and so they got through in peace.

Neither spoke until they were in a silent lane again.

"Sometimes they can be quite disagreeable," he said, "but it is amusing to see it all. The Sheikh lives here, he fancies the pyramids belong to him, just as the Khedive fancies all Egypt is his."

Now Tamara could see his face better as he looked up to her superior height on the camel. He had a little moustache and peculiarly chiselled lips, too chiselled for a man, she thought for a moment, until she noticed the firm jaw.

His eyes were sleepy, slightly Oriental in their setting, and looked very dark, and yet something made her think that in daylight they might be blue or grey.

He did not smile at all; as he spoke his face

8

was grave, but when something made him laugh as they turned the next corner, it transformed him. It was the rippling spontaneous gaiety of a child.

Two goats had got loose from opposite hovels and were butting at each other in the middle of the road.

He pulled up his horse and watched.

"I like any fight," he said.

But the goats fled in fear of him, so they went on.

Tamara was wondering why she felt so stupid. She wanted to ask her strange companion a number of questions.

Who he was? What he was doing at the Sphinx, and indeed in Egypt?

Why had he spoken to her at all, and yet appeared absolutely indifferent as they rode along? He had not asked her a single question or expressed the least curiosity. For some reason she felt piqued.

Presently they emerged at the end of the village where there was a small lake left by the retirement of the Nile. The moon, almost full, was mirrored in it.

The scene was one of extreme beauty. The pyramids appeared an old rose-pink, and everything else in tones of sapphire, not the green-blue of moonlight in other countries.

All was breathlessly still and lifeless. Only they two, and the camel boys, alone in the night.

"You are going to the hotel, I suppose?" he said. "I will see you safely to it."

"And you?" Tamara could not prevent herself from asking. "Where do you go?"

"To hell, sometimes," he answered, and his eyes were full of mist, "but tonight I shall go to bed for a change."

Tamara was nonplussed. She felt intensely commonplace. She was even a little cross with herself. Why had she asked a question?

The Arab horse now took it into his head to curvet and bound in the air for no apparent reason, but the young man did not stir an inch, he only laughed.

"Go on, my beauty," he said. "I like you to be so spirited. It shows you are alive."

As they approached the hotel, Tamara began to hope no one would see them. No one who could tell Millicent that she had a companion.

She bent down and said rather primly to the young man who was again at her side:

"I am quite safe now, thank you. I need not trouble you any further. Good-bye! I am so obliged to you for showing me a new way home."

He looked up at her, and his whole face was lit up with a whimsical smile.

"Don't be nervous. I will go at the gate."

Tamara did not speak, and presently they came to the turning into the hotel.

"I suppose we shall meet again someday," he said. "They have a proverb here, 'Meet before dawn—part not till dawn.' They see into the future in a few drops of water in any hollow thing. Good-night."

Before she could answer he was off beyond the hotel up the road and turning to the right on a sand-path, galloping out of sight into what must be the vast desert.

Where on earth could he be going to? Possibly the devil!

* * *

When Tamara woke in the morning the recollection of her camel ride seemed like a dream. She sat for a long time at the window of her room, looking out towards the green world and Cairo.

She was trying to adjust things in her mind. This stranger had certainly left an impression on her.

She wondered who he was, and how he would look in daylight. Then she wondered at herself. The whole thing was so bizarre in a life of carefully balanced proprieties.

She was very sensitive, and she felt he had laughed at her prim propriety in wishing to get rid of him before the gate.

Indeed, she suddenly felt he might laugh at a good many of the things she did.

"You haven't told me a thing about your Sphinx excursion last night, Tamara," Millicent Hardcastle said at breakfast, rather peevishly.

They were sipping coffee together in the latter's room.

"Was it nice, and had the tourists quite departed?"

"It was wonderful!" Tamara replied. "There were no tourists, and it made me think a number of new things. We seem such ordinary people, Millicent."

Mrs Hardcastle glanced up, surprised.

"You may wonder, but it is true, Milly," she went on, "we do the same things every day, and think the same thoughts, and are just thoroughly commonplace and uninteresting."

"And you came to these conclusions from gazing at the Sphinx?" Mrs Hardcastle asked.

"Yes," said Tamara, the pink deepening for a moment in her cheeks.

In her whole life she had hardly ever had a secret.

"I sat here, Millicent, in the sand opposite that strange image, and it seemed to smile and mock at all little things."

After breakfast they started for a last donkey ride, as they must return to Cairo in time for the Khedive's ball that night, to which they were being taken by their compatriots at the Embassy.

Tomorrow they were to return to Europe. Mrs Hardcastle could not spare more time away from her babies. Their visit had only been of four short weeks, and now it was December 27, and home and husband called her.

For Tamara's part, she could do as she pleased; indeed, for two pins she would have stayed on in Egypt.

But that was not the intention of fate!

"Do let us go up that sand-path, Millicent," she said when they turned out of the hotel gate. "We have never been there, and I would like to see where it leads to; perhaps we shall get quite a new vista from the top."

What she expected to find she did not ask herself. In any case they rode on, eventually coming out at a small enclosure where there was a bungalow.

Tamara had vaguely observed it in the distance, but imagined it to be some water-tower of the hotel, it was so bare and gaunt.

It was a quaint place with tiny windows high up, evidently to light a studio, and there was a verandah to look at the view towards the Nile.

When they got fairly close they could see that on this verandah a young man was stretched at full length.

Tamara was conscious that the young man was only clothed in blue and white striped silk pyjamas, the jacket of which was open and showed his chest, and one foot, stretched out and hanging over the back of another low chair, was actually bare!

Mrs Hardcastle touched her donkey and hurried past, the path went so very near this unseemly sight!

Tamara followed, but not before the young man had time to raise himself and frown with fury. She almost imagined she heard him saying-ing:

"Those devils of tourists!"

She glowed with annoyance. Did he think she had come to look at him?

He was certainly quite uninterested, for he must have recognised her! But perhaps not; people look do different in large straw hats from what they do with scarves of chiffon tied over their heads.

But why had she come this way at all? She wished a thousand times she had suggested going round the pyramids instead.

"Tamara," Mrs Hardcastle said, "did you see there was a *man* in that chair? What a dreadful person to be lying on the balcony undressed!"

"I never noticed," said Tamara, without a blush. "I am surprised at you having looked, Millie, when this view is so fine."

"But, my dear child, I could not possibly help seeing him. How you did not notice I can't think; he had pyjamas on, Tamara, and *bare feet!*"

Mrs Hardcastle almost whispered the last terrible words.

"I suppose he felt hot," said Tamara; "it is a grilling day."

"But really, dear, no nice people, in any weather, remain undressed at twelve o'clock in the day for passers-by to look at, do they?"

"Well, perhaps he isn't a nice person," allowed Tamara. "He may be mad. What was he like, since you saw so much, Millicent?"

Mrs Hardcastle glanced over her shoulder reproachfully.

"You really speak as though I had looked on purpose," she said. "He seemed very long. I suppose, as his hair was not very dark, he must be an Englishman."

"Oh, dear, no!" exclaimed Tamara. "Not an Englishman!"

Then, seeing her friend's expression of surprise:

"I mean, it isn't likely an Englishman would lie on his balcony in pyjamas, at least not the ones we see in Cairo; they are too busy, aren't they?"

"Possibly it was a madman, Tamara, sent here with a keeper, in that out-of-the-way place. How fortunate we had the donkey boys with us!"

Tamara laughed.

"You dear goose, Millie, he couldn't have eaten us up you know; and he was not doing the least harm. We should not have gone that way; it may have been his private path."

"Still, no one should lie about undressed," Mrs Hardcastle protested. "It is not at all nice. Girls might have been riding with us, and how dreadful it would have been then."

"Let us forget it!" Tamara laughed, "and get some real exercise."

So off they started at a trot.

Just as they were turning out of the hotel gate, late in the same afternoon, a young man on an Arabian horse passed the carriage. He was in ordinary riding dress, and looked a slim, graceful sight as they trotted ahead.

He never glanced their way. But while Tamara felt a sudden emotion she could not repress, Mrs Hardcastle exclaimed:

"Look, look! I am sure that is the madman who wore those pyjamas!"

Chapter
Two

The Khedive's ball was a fine sight. The palace was decorated in the style of the Third French Empire.

The levee uniforms of the officers gave an air of brilliance contrasted with those of the civilians of the Government of Egypt.

Tamara found herself whirling with a gay Hussar.

"Let us stop near the Royalties and look at the Russians," he said. "You know, a Grand Duke arrived today, and will be here tonight."

They came to a standstill close to the little group surrounding the Khedive, and amid the splendid uniforms of the Grand Duke's suite there was one of scarlet.

Tamara learnt it was a Cossack of the Emperor's Escort, but at the moment it seemed like a gorgeous fancy dress.

The high boots and long, strangely graceful coat, the white under-dress, the way the loose scarlet sleeves fell at the wrist, the gold and silver trimmings, all pleased her eye extremely.

Then she recognised its wearer as the young man of the Sphinx. He looked now, in this gorgeous garment, very much a Prince in a fairy tale.

He did not appear to see her, but when she began dancing again, and paused once more for breath, she was close to him as he stood some way apart and alone.

Their eyes met. His had the same whimsical provoking smile in them which angered and yet attracted her. He made no move to bow to her, nor did he take any steps to be introduced. She burnt with annoyance.

"He might at least have been presented; it is too impertinent otherwise!" she thought.

She knew she was looking her best; a fair, distinguished woman as young and fresh as a girl. Hardly a man in the room was unconscious of her presence.

Anger lent an extra brightness to her eyes and cheeks. She went on dancing wildly.

The next time she was near the stranger was half an hour later, although not once was she able to banish the scarlet form from her view.

He did not dance. He talked now and then to his Prince, and then he was presented to the official ladies, with the rest of the suite. He looked bored.

Tamara would not ask his name, which she could have done with ease, as everyone was interested in the Russians, and glad to talk about them.

She avoided the English group of bigwigs where they were standing. And when they passed the tall Cossack again she turned upon him a witheringly unconscious glance.

Presently she was requested by one of the attachés to come and be presented to the Grand Duke, and when she had made her curtsy it was the turn of his suite.

"Prince Milaslavski," and she heard one of his friends call him "Gritzko."

The name fell pleasantly on her ears, but why was he such a wretch as to humiliate her? She felt horribly small. She ought never to have let him speak to her at the Sphinx. She was being thoroughly punished now for her unconventionality.

She said a few words in French to each of the others, and then, as he still stood there with that provoking smile in his splendid eyes, she turned away, almost biting her lip with shame and rage.

Then a voice said close to her ear:

"May I have the honour of a dance, Madame?"

She looked up into the eyes of the Prince, and for a second she hesitated. Her first impulse was to say No, but she quickly realised that would be undignified and absurd.

She said "Yes," coldly, and let him place his arm about her. The band was playing a particularly sensuous valse, and his movements were heaven!

Tamara did not speak a word. She purposely did not look at him, but drooped her proud head so that the flashing diamonds of her tiara were all he could see of her.

He put no special meaning into the way he held her; he just danced divinely; but there was something in the creature himself of a perfectly annoying attractiveness, or so it seemed to Tamara.

They at last paused for a moment, and then he spoke.

He made not the slightest allusion to the Sphinx incident. He spoke gravely of Cairo, and the polo, and the races, and said that his Grand Duke had arrived that day.

He was not on his staff, but was travelling in Egypt for his own amusement. He had been there since November, had been up the Nile, and had fortunately been able to secure a little bungalow at Mena, where he could spend some hours of peace.

Then Tamara laughed.

She remembered Millicent Hardcastle's consternation over those unfortunate pyjamas. She wondered if Millicent would realise that she was dancing with their wearer now!

When she laughed he put his arm round her once more and began dancing. This time he held her rather close.

Suddenly as she laughed again to herself provokingly, he clasped her tight.

"If you laugh like that I will kiss you here in the room," he said.

Tamara stopped dead. She blazed with anger.

"How dare you be so impertinent?"

They were up in a corner; everyone's backs were turned to them, and in one second he bent and kissed her neck.

It was done with such incredible swiftness and audacity that even if he had been observed it would only have looked as if he bent to pick up something she had dropped.

But the kiss burnt into Tamara's flesh.

She could hardly keep the tears of outraged pride from her eyes.

"How dare you! How dare you!" she hissed. "You are making me ashamed of having let you speak to me last night!"

"Last night?" he said.

Her forcibly drew her hand within his arm and began walking towards the group of her friends.

"Last night you were afraid someone should see me from the hotel, and tonight you dare me. Do it once more and I will kiss your lips!"

Tamara went white; she felt as if the ground were sinking beneath her feet; her knees trembled. In all her smooth, conventionally ordered life she had never experienced such emotions.

The Prince glanced at her, and the fierceness went out of his eyes. He bowed gravely with the most courtly homage, and left her standing by Millicent's side.

"Thank God!" she said to herself, when a few hours later she got into bed. "Thank God we are going away tomorrow! I shall never see him again, and no one will ever know!"

* * *

Next day they started. Their compartment was a bower of flowers, and as each moment went by Tamara's equanimity was restored by the thought that she would soon be out of the land of her disgrace.

They hurried on board the ship when they arrived in Alexandria.

Neither woman was a good sailor, and both were overcome with fatigue.

The next day, which was Sunday, the wind blew, but by the afternoon calmed down again, and Tamara decided to dress and go on deck.

Her maid preceded her with her rug and cushion and book, and it was not until she was quite settled that she found her friend in the next chair.

"You lazy child!" Millicent Hardcastle said. "To sleep all day like this! It has been quite beautiful since luncheon, and I have had a most agreeable time.

"That extremely polite nice young Russian Prince we met at the Khedive's ball is here, indeed that is his chair next to yours. He is with Stephen Strong. We have been talking for hours."

Tamara felt suddenly almost cold.

"I never saw him in the train or coming on board," she said, with almost a gasp.

"Nor did I. Our places at meals are next him, too. So fortunate he was introduced, because one could not talk to a strange man, even on a boat."

Tamara was pondering what to do. She could not decline to know the Prince without making some explanation to Millicent. She must just be icily cold, and if he should be further impertinent she could remain in her cabin.

But what an annoying contretemps! And she had thought she should never see him again!

Now she would be constantly reminded of the most disgraceful incident in her career.

She had half an hour to grow calm before the cause of her unrest came even into sight, and when he did, it was to walk past in the company of their old friend Stephen Strong.

The Prince raised his cap gravely. She felt she must have a little fun with Millicent.

"Has it struck you, Millie, the Prince is the same young man we saw in the pyjamas on the verandah? I am surprised at your speaking to such a person, even if he has been introduced!"

"Really, Tamara," she said. "I had altogether forgotten that unpleasant incident. I wish you had not reminded me of it. He is a most respectful, modest, unassuming young man. I am sure he would be dreadfully uncomfortable if he were aware we had seen him."

"Hush! He is coming towards us." Tamara hurriedly opened a book and looked down.

"At last, Mrs. Loraine has arrived on deck," she heard Millicent say; and for convention's sake, she was obliged to glance up and bow coldly.

The Prince did not seem the least impressed; he sat down and pulled his rug round his knees and gazed out at the sea. The sun had set, and the moon would soon rise in all her full glory.

Tamara pretended to read her book, but she was conscious of his proximity. Nothing so magnetic in the way of a personality had ever crossed her path before.

He sat as still as a statue, gazing at the sea. An uncontrollable desire to look at him shook

Tamara, but she dominated it. The discomfort at last grew so great that she almost trembled.

"Have you cat's eyes?" he asked.

Now, when there was a legitimate chance to look at him, she glued her eyes to her book.

"Of course not!" she replied icily.

"Then of what use to pretend you are reading in this gloom?"

Tamara was silent. She even turned a page. She would be irritating too!

"That ball was a sight," he continued. "Did you see the harem ladies peeping from their cage? They looked fat and ugly enough to be wisely kept there. What a lot of fools they must have thought us, cavorting for their amusement."

"Poor women!" Tamara said.

"Why poor women?" he asked. "They have all the pleasures of the body, and no anxieties; nothing but the little excitement of trying now and then to poison their rivals! Poor Khedive! Think of him having to wade through all that fat mass to find one pretty one!"

The tone of this conversation displeased Tamara. She wished he would be silent again, only that deep voice of his was so pleasant!

She did allow herself to look at him because she could not help admiring the way his hair grew, back from a forehead purely Greek. His nose was short and rather square, while his too-beautifully chiselled lips had an expression of extraordinary charm.

His whole personality breathed attraction; every human being who approached him was conscious of it.

As for his eyes, they were enormous, with

broad, full lids, mystical, passionate, and yet un-concerned. They suggested something Eastern, though on the whole he was fair.

Tamara's own soft brown hair was only a shade lighter than his. She was not sure yet, but now thought his eyes were grey.

She could have asked him a number of ques-tions she wanted answered, but she refrained. He suddenly turned and looked at her full in the face.

He had been gazing fixedly at the sea, and these movements of quickness were disconcerting, especially as Tamara found herself caught in the act of studying his features.

"What on earth made you go to the Sphinx?" he asked.

"To count the number of stones the creature is made of, of course," she replied. "Those tech-nical things are what one would go for at that time of night."

And now her companion rippled with laugh-ter, infectious joyous laughter.

"Ah, you are not so stupid as I thought!" he said, frankly. "You looked so poetic with that gauze scarf round your head, then afterwards. Wheugh! You were like a pretty wax doll. I re-gretted having wasted the village on you. It is full of meaning for me."

Tamara was interested in spite of her will to remain reserved, although she resented the "wax doll."

"Yes?" she faltered.

"You can learn all the lessons you want in life from the Sphinx," he went on. "She is cruel, and does not hesitate to tear one in pieces if she wishes, and she could make one ready to get drunk on blood."

Tamara's eyes were round.

"Then the village there, full of men with the passions of animals, wailing for a death, rejoicing at a birth, taking strong physical pleasure in their marriage rights. Beating their women when they are tired; but you are too civilised in your country to understand any of these things."

Tamara was stirred; she felt she ought to be shocked.

"Then you are not civilised in yours?" she asked.

"The primitive forces of life still give us emotions, when we are not wild," he replied. "When we are, then it is the jolliest hell."

Tamara was almost repulsed. How could anyone be so odd as this man?

Was he a type, or was he mad, or just only most annoyingly attractive and different from anyone else? She found herself thrilled.

With a stubtle change he turned and almost tenderly wrapped the rug, which had slipped a little, more securely round her.

"You have such a small white face," he said, the words a caress. "One must see that you are warm and the naughty winds do not blow you away."

Tamara shivered; she could not have told why.

After this the conversation became general. Millicent joined in with her obvious remarks.

Something angered Tamara in the way the Prince replied, outcommonplacing her friend in commonplaces with the suavest politeness, while

25

his face betrayed him not even by a twinkle in the eye.

Only when he caught hers; then he laughed a sudden short laugh, and he whispered:

"What a perfect woman! Everything in the right place. Heaven! She would do her knitting, and hand one a child every year! I'll marry when I can find a wife like that!"

Tamara was furious. She resented his ridicule of Millicent, and she was horrified at the whole speech; so, gathering her rug together, she said she was cold, and asked Mr Strong to pace the deck with her.

At dinner the Prince seemed to be practically a stranger again. He was Tamara's neighbour, but he risked no startling speeches.

In fact he hardly spoke to her, contenting himself with discussing seafaring matters with the Captain, and an occasional remark to Stephen Strong.

She had decided to snub him; he did not give her her chance.

* * *

On Monday they heard they would arrive at Brindisi on Tuesday morning, and Tamara persuaded Mrs Hardcastle to agree to disembarking there instead of going on to Trieste.

"We shall be home all the sooner," she said.

It was a perfect day, the blue Mediterranean was not belying its name, and Tamara felt in great spirits, as she came on deck at about eleven o'clock.

She found Millicent taking a vigorous walk round and round with the Russian Prince. They seemed to be laughing and chattering like old friends.

Tamara resented it.

"He is only making fun of poor Millie, who never sees a thing," she thought.

She settled herself in her chair and let her eyes feast on the blue sea. What should she do with her life? This taste of change and foreign skies had unsettled her.

How could she return to Underwood and the humdrum everyday existence there? She seemed to realise that always there had been dormant in her some difference from the others.

"Next summer I shall be twenty-five years old," she said to herself, "and the whole thing has been a waste."

Presently Stephen Strong came up and took Mrs Hardcastle's chair.

"May I disturb your meditations?" he said. "You look so wise."

"No, I am foolish," Tamara answered. "You who know the world must come and talk and teach me its meaning."

"The world," he said, as he arranged himself in the chair, "is an extremely pleasant place if one takes it as it is, and does not quarrel with it. See it all and make allowances for the weakness of the human beings who inhabit it."

"I know you are right," Tamara replied, "but so many of us belong to a tribe who think their point of view the only one. For instance, I do, that is why I say I am foolish."

The walkers passed again.

"There is a type for you to study," Stephen

Strong said. "Prince Milaslavski. I have known him for many years, since he was a child almost; he is about twenty-nine or thirty now, and really a rather interesting personality."

"Yes," said Tamara, honestly, "I feel that. Tell me about him!"

"He came into his vast fortune rather too young, and lived rather fiercely. His mother was a Basmanoff; which means a kind of Croesus in Russia.

"He is a great favourite and is in the Cossacks of the Escort. Something in their wild freedom appealed to him. He is a Cossack himself on the mother's side, and the blood is wild."

Tamara looked interested.

"They tell the most tremendous stories about him," the old man went on, "hugely exaggerated, of course; but the fact remains, he is a fascinating, restless, dauntless character."

"What sort of stories?" Tamara asked timidly.

"Not all fit for your ears, gentle lady," laughed Stephen Strong. "Sheer devilment, mostly. He ran off with a nun once, it is said, for a bet, and deposited her in the house of the man she had loved before her vows were taken.

"He has orgies sometimes at his country place, when everyone is mad for three days on end. It causes a terrible scandal. Then he comes back like a lamb and purrs to all the old ladies. They say he obeys neither God nor the Devil, only the Emperor on this earth."

"How dreadful!" force of habit made Tamara say, while her thoughts unconsciously ran into interested fascination.

28

"He is absolutely fearless," Stephen Strong continued, "and indeed sometimes he lives the simplest country life with his horses and dogs, and his own people worship him, I believe. But there is no wildest prank he is incapable of if his blood is up."

"I think he looks wild," Tamara murmured.

"If you could see him in Petersburg, then I believe you would be like all the rest."

"All which rest?" asked Tamara.

"Women. They simply adore him. Bohemians, great ladies, actresses, dancers."

Something in her rose up in arms.

"It shows how foolish they are," she said.

Stephen Strong glanced at her sideways, and if she could have read his thoughts they were:

"This sweet Englishwoman is under Gritzko's spell already, and how she is battling against it! She won't have a chance, though, if he makes up his mind to win."

But Tamara, for all her gentle features, was no weakling.

"What can he be talking about to my friend, Mr Strong?" she asked, as the two passed again.

"He always does the unexpected," Stephen Strong laughed. He himself was amused at this ill-matched pair.

"Mrs Hardcastle is agreeable to look at."

Tamara smiled scornfully.

"That is the lowest view to take. One should see above the material appearance."

"Charming lady!" said Stephen Strong. "Yes, indeed you do not know the world."

Tamara was not angry. She looked at him and smiled, showing her beautiful teeth.

"Of course you think me a goose," she said, "but I warned you I was one. Tell me, shall I ever grow out of it?"

"If the teacher is young and handsome enough to make your heart beat," said her companion.

Then Millicent and the Prince joined them. Mrs Hardcastle's round blue eyes were flashing brightly, and her fresh face was aglow with exercise and enjoyment.

"Tamara dear, you are too incorrigibly lazy. Why do you sit here instead of taking exercise? And you have no idea of the interesting things the Prince has been telling me.

"All about a Russian poet called . . . oh, I can't pronounce the name, but who wrote of a devil."

Tamara noticed that amused, whimsical mocking gleam in the Cossack's great eyes, but Millicent went gaily on.

"I mean those mythical, strange sort of devils who come to earth, you know, and make love to ladies, a sort of Satan, like in Marie Corelli's lovely book. You remember, Tamara, the one you were so funny about, when you read it."

"You mean *The Demon* of Lermontoff, don't you?" Tamara asked.

"You know our great poet's work, then?" the Prince said in surprise. "One would not have thought it!"

Again Tamara's anger rose. There was always the insinuation in his remarks, seemingly unconscious, and therefore the more irritating, that she was a commonplace fool.

"The heroine's name is the same as my own," she said, gravely; but there was a challenge in her eyes.

"Tamara!" he exclaimed. "Well, a devil might come your way, but you would kneel, pray, eat bonbons, and not listen to him."

"It would depend upon the devil," she said. "Those who live the longest will see the most."

The Prince put back his head and laughed with real enjoyment at his thoughts.

Tamara felt her cheeks blaze with rage, and again took up her book.

"No, don't read," the Prince said. "You get angry with me when we talk, and the colour comes into your cheeks, and I like it."

Exasperation was almost uncontrollable in Tamara. She remained silent, only the little ear next to the Prince burnt scarlet.

"Someday you will come to Russia," he said, "and then you will learn many things."

"I have no desire to go there," Tamara lied, as it had always been her great wish, and indeed her godmother, who never forgot her, had often begged her to visit that northern clime.

"It would freeze you, perhaps, or burn you, who can tell?" the Prince said. "One would see when you got there. I have an old lady, a dear friend, with white hair and a mole on her cheek, someone who sees straight. She would be good for your education."

Tamara thought it would be wiser not to show any further annoyance, so she said mockingly.

"I am only sixteen, and have never left the schoolroom; it would be delightful to be taught how to live."

He turned and smiled at her.

"You hardly look any more, twenty perhaps, and never kissed!"

A memory rose up of a scorched neck, and suddenly Tamara's long eyelashes rested on her cheek.

Then into his splendid eyes came a fierce, savage, passionate gleam, which she did not see, but dimly felt, and he said in a low voice a little thick:

"And, as yet, never really kissed."

* * *

The Prince did not come in to luncheon, something was the matter with his Arabian horse, and he had gone to see to it, with concern on his face.

About tea-time he turned up again.

"He is all right now," he said. "It was those fools down there, I have made them suffer."

He turned to Stephen Strong.

"Among the steerage there is an Alexandrian gipsy troupe. I have ordered them to sing to us to-night, since Madame wished it."

He turned to Millicent with an air of deep devotion.

"Common ragged creatures, but one with some ankles and one with a voice. In any case, we must celebrate these ladies' last night."

Nothing could have been more charming than the Prince was until dinner-time, and indeed throughout the meal.

He made Stephen Strong change places

with him, so that he might be next Mrs Hard-castle, much to that lady's delight.

"He is really too fascinating," she said as she came into Tamara's cabin. "I hardly think Henry would like his devotion to me. What do you think, dear?"

"I am sure he would be awfully jealous, Milly darling; you really must be careful," Tamara replied.

It was not possible, she thought, that anything so terribly unpleasant as the Prince's having too much champagne at dinner could have accounted for his simply sandalous behaviour afterwards.

Yet surely that would have been the kindest thing to say. But, no, it was not that.

With the permission of the Captain, the gipsy troupe were brought, and began their performance, tame enough at the commencement until the Prince gave orders for them to be supplied with unlimited champagne, and then the wildest dancing began.

They writhed and gesticulated and undulated in a manner which made Millicent cling on to her chair, crimson in the face, and finally start to her feet.

But the worst happened when the Prince rose and, taking a tambourine, began, with a weird shriek, to beat it wildly, his eyes ablaze.

Then, seizing the chief dancer and banging it upon her head, he held his arm about her heaving breast, as she turned to him with a serpentine movement of voluptuous delight.

In a second he had caught hold of her and had lifted and swung her far out over the dark

33

blue waters; then, with a swirl to the side, held her suspended in the air above the open deck below.

The troupe yelled in frenzied pleasure, and, nimble as a cat, one rough dark man rushed down the ladder and caught the hanging woman in his arms.

Then they all clapped and cheered and shrieked with joy, while the Prince, putting his hands in his pockets, pulled out heaps of gold and flung it among them.

"Back to hell, rats!" he shouted, laughing. "See, you have frightened the ladies. You should all be killed!"

For Tamara and Millicent had risen, and with stately steps had quitted the scene.

It was all too terrible and too vulgarly melodramatic, Tamara thought, especially the touching of the woman and the flinging of gold.

The next morning they left the ship at Brindisi before either the Prince or Stephen Strong was awake.

Both were silent upon the subject of the night before, until Millicent at last said when they were in the train:

"Tamara, you won't tell Henry, or your family, will you, dear? Last night, he was so fascinating, but that dancing! I am sure you feel, with me, we could have died of shame!"

Chapter
Three

When Tamara reached Underwood and saw a letter from her Russian godmother among the pile which awaited her, she felt it was the finger of fate.

She read it and found it contained not only New Year's wishes, but an invitation couched in affectionate and persuasive terms that she should visit St. Petersburg.

Suddenly, and without consulting her family, she decided she would go.

"There is something drawing me to Russia," she said to herself. "Why should I not accept, just because one Russian man has horrified me? It is, I suppose, a big city, and perhaps I shall never see him there."

So she announced her decision to the dumb-founded household, and in less than a week took the Nord Express.

"The Court, alas! is in mourning," her god-mother had written, "so you will see no splendid Court balls, but I dare say we can divert you otherwise, and I am so anxious to make the acquaintance of my godchild."

Tamara speeding on her way to the North found her interest and excitement deepening with each mile of the journey.

The snow and the vast forests impressed her from the train windows. She was sensitive to all form and colour.

The silence seemed to be the first thing she remarked on reaching the frontier. The porters were so grave and quiet, their bearded kindly faces like the saints and Biblical characters.

Finally she arrived at St. Petersburg, and found her godmother waiting for her on the platform. They recognised each other immediately. Tamara had several photographs of the Princess Ardacheff.

"Welcome, *ma filleule*," that lady cried, while she shook her head. "After all these years I can have you in my house."

They said all sorts of mutually agreeable things on their way and looked at each other shyly.

"She is beautiful," ran the Princess's comments. "And she has a superb air of breeding, that is from her poor mother, but her eyes are her father's. She is very sweet, and what a lovely skin."

Tamara thought:

"My godmother is a splendid-looking lady! I like her brown bright eyes and white hair. What a queer black mole upon her left cheek, like an early-eighteenth-century beauty spot. Where have I heard lately of someone with a mole . . . ?"

"You fortunately see our city with a fresh mantle of snow, Tamara," the Princess said, glancing from the automobile window as they sped along. "It is not, alas! always so white as this."

It appeared wonderful to Tamara, quite unlike anything she had imagined. The tiny sleighs seemed too ridiculously small for the enormously padded coachmen on the boxes.

Her first remark was almost a childish one of glee and appreciation, and then she stopped short. What would her godmother think of such an outburst?

The Princess Ardacheff's frank face was illuminated with a smile.

"She is extremely young, in spite of her widowhood," she thought, "but I like her, and I know we shall be friends."

Just then they arrived at her house in the Surguiefskaia. It had not appeared to Tamara that they were approaching any particularly fashionable quarter.

When they entered the first hall and the gaily liveried suisse and two footmen removed their furs, and the Princess's snow boots, Tamara perceived she was indeed in a glorious home.

Princess Ardacheff's house was, in fact, the most stately in all Petersburg.

As they ascended the enormous staircase dividing on the first landing, and reaching the surrounding galleries above in two sweeps, a grave Major-domo and more footmen met them.

They opened wide the doors of a lofty room. It was full of fine pictures and *objets d'art*, and the furniture dated from the time of Alexander II, and even a little earlier.

Tea and quantities of different little *bonnes*

bounches awaited them. But if there was a samo-
var Tamara did not recognise it.

The Princess talked in a fashion of perfect
simplicity and directness. She told her that her
friends would all welcome her and be glad that
an Englishwoman should really see their country,
and find it was not at all the grotesque place it
had often been painted.

"We are so far away that you do not even
imagine us," she said. "You English have read
that there was an Ivan the Terrible and a Peter
the Great.

"Many of you believe wolves prowl in the
streets at night, and that among the highest
society nihilists stalk, disguised as heaven knows
what!"

She laughed and continued.

"While the sudden disappearance of a member of any great or small family can be accounted for by a nocturnal visit of police, and a
transportation in chains to Siberia mines! Is it
not so, Tamara?"

"Yes, indeed," she replied. "I am sure that
is what Aunt Clara thinks now! Are we not a
ridiculously insular people, *Marraine?*"

She said the last word timidly and put out
her hand.

"May I call you *Marraine*, Princess?" she
asked. "I never knew my mother, and it sounds
nice."

"Indeed, yes!" the Princess said, and she
rose and kissed Tamara. "Your mother was very
dear to me; before you were born, we spent a
wild season together of youth and happiness.

You shall take the place of my child if she had lived."

Before they had finished drinking their tea, other guests came in. A tall old General in a beautiful uniform, and two ladies, one young and the other old. They all spoke English perfectly.

Presently she heard the elder lady say to her godmother:

"Have you seen Gritzko since his return, Vera? One hears he has a wild fit on and is at Milaslav with . . ." the rest of the words were whispered.

Tamara found herself unpleasantly on the alert. How ridiculous though, she thought. There might be a dozen Gritzkos in Petersburg.

"No, he returns tonight," Princess Ardacheff said, "but I never listen to these tales, and as no matter what he does we all forgive him, and let him fly back into our good graces as soon as he purses up that handsome mouth of his!"

The lady appeared to agree to this, for she laughed, and they talked of other things, and soon all left.

"Tonight I have one or two of my nicest friends dining," the Princess said, "whom I wish you to know, so I thought if you rested now you would not be too tired for a little society."

The company, ten or twelve of them, were all assembled when Tamara reached one of the great Salons, which opened from the galleries surrounding the marble hall.

She came in, a slender willowy creature with a gentle smile of contrition.

Then the presentations took place. What

struck her first was that dark or fair, fat-faced or thin, high foreheads or low, all the ladies wore *coiffes* exactly the same; the hair brushed up from the forehead.

It gave a look of universal distinction, but in some cases was not very becoming. They were beautifully dressed in black, and before the end of the evening Tamara felt she had never met women with such charm.

Surely no other country could produce the same types. Extremely highly educated, with a wide range of subjects, and a knowledge of European literature which was unsurpassed.

It seemed to Tamara that each one was endowed with natural fascination. There were no gushing compliments. They were just casual and delightful and made her feel at home and happy with them all.

They took *Zacouska* in an ante-room, where there were quantities of strange dishes! There seemed enough for a whole meal, and Tamara wondered how it would be possible to eat anything further!

At dinner she sat between a tall old Prince and a diplomat. The uniforms pleased her and the glorious pearls of the ladies.

The pretty custom of the men kissing the hostess's hand as they all left the dining-room together, she found delightful.

They were drinking coffee in the Blue Salon. Most of the party had retired to the bridge tables, and Tamara was sitting by the fire with her godmother and another lady.

Suddenly, the door opened and with an air

of complete insouciance and assurance, Prince Milaslavski came in.

"I want some coffee, *Tantine*," he said, kissing the Princess's hand, while he nodded to everyone else.

"Gritzko—back again!" the whole company cried, and the Princess, beaming upon him fond smiles, gave him the coffee, while she murmured a glad welcome.

"That old cat of a Marianne Mariuski has set about as usual one of her stories. I am having an orgy at Milaslav, and this time with a seraglio of Egyptian houris. The truth is I only brought back by the merest chance one small troupe of Alexandrian dancers and two performing bears."

"Gritzko, will you never learn wisdom," said one lady, the Princess Shebanoff, plaintively, while the others all laughed.

"*Tantine*," the Prince exclaimed, "you have not presented me to the English lady, who is, I perceive, a stranger."

Tamara sat cold and silent. She was angry with herself that this man's entrance should cause her such emotion, or rather commotion and sensation.

Why should he make her feel nervous and stupid, unsure of herself, and uncertain what to do?

Invariably he placed her at some disadvantage, and left the settling of their relations to himself. Whereas all such regulations ought to have been in her hands.

Now she could only bow stiffly as her godmother said his name and hers. Prince Milaslavski took a chair by her side and began making politesses as though he were really a stranger.

Had she just arrived? Did she find Russia very cold? Was she going to stay long? etcetera, etcetera.

To all of which Tamara answered in monosyllables, while two bright spots of rose colour burnt in her cheeks.

The Prince was astonishingly good-looking in his Cossack's uniform, and his eyes had a laugh in them.

His whole manner to Tamara was different. It was as if a courtly Russian were welcoming an honoured guest in his aunt's house.

He did not mock or tease, or announce startling truths; he was pleasant, ordinary, and serene.

He and the Princess Ardacheff were not real blood relations; the first wife of her late husband had been his mother's sister, but the tradition of aunt had gone on in the family and the Princess loved him almost as a son.

"What did you think of Gritzko Milaslavski, Tamara?" she asked, when all the guests were gone, and the two had retired to Tamara's room. "He is one of the dearest characters when you know him . . . but a terrible tease."

"He seemed very pleasant," Tamara said blankly.

Even to speak of him caused her unease.

"He is not at all the type of an ordinary Russian," the Princess continued. "He has travelled so much."

Then she kissed her goddaughter good-night, and she said:

"You were not shocked about the Alexandrian dancers, I hope, child?" she said. "If one knew the truth, they probably were poor people who were starving, Gritzko would help them out of the kindness of his heart."

Tamara, left to herself, gazed into the glowing embers of her wood fire.

"I wonder . . . I wonder," she murmured.

* * *

The next day was the last of the Russian old year, the twelfth of January new style, and when Tamara appeared about ten o'clock in her godmother's own sitting-room, she found the Princess already busy at her writing table.

"Good-morning, my child," she said. "You behold me up and working at a time when most of my countrywomen are not yet in their baths. We keep late hours here in the winter, while it is dark and cold.

"You will get accustomed to going to bed at two and rising at ten; but tonight I fear it will be four in the morning before you sleep.

"Prince Milaslavski has telephoned that he gives a party at his house on the Fontonka, to dine first and then go on to a cafe to hear the Bohemians sing. It is a peculiarity of the place, these Bohemians, and we shall drink in the New Year."

She took up the telephone by her side.

"It is you, Gritzko? Awake? Of course she is awake, and here in the room. Yes, it is arranged, we will dine at nine o'clock? Now promise you will be good. Any English lady would be shocked at you. I tell you she is in the room, so pray be more discreet."

She smiled at Tamara, and then continued her conversation.

"No, I will not talk in Russian, it is very rude. If you are not proper at dinner we will not go on. I am serious! Good-bye."

With a laugh the Princess put the receiver down.

"He says nothing would shock you, he is sure you understand the world! Well, we must amuse ourselves and try and restrain him if he grows too wild."

"He is often wild, then?" Tamara asked.

The Princess rose and stood by the window, looking out on the thickly falling snow.

"I am afraid, a little, though never in the wrong situation; above all things Gritzko is a gentleman; but sometimes I wish he would take life less as a game. One cannot help speculating how it can end."

"Has he no family?" Tamara asked.

"No, everyone is dead. His mother worshipped him, but she died when he was scarcely eighteen, and his father before that. His mother is his adored memory.

"In all the mad scenes which he and his companions have enacted in the Fontonka house, there is one set of rooms no one has dared to enter, he keeps flowers there, and an ever-burning lamp."

She paused.

"There is a strange touch of sentiment and melancholy in Gritzko, and of religion too. Sometimes I think he is unhappy, and then he goes off to his castle in the Caucasus or to Milaslav, and no one sees him for weeks.

"One must accept him as he is, or leave him alone, he will go his own way."

Tamara had ceased fighting with herself about the interest she took in conversations relating to the Prince.

She could not restrain her desire to hear of him, but she explained it now by telling herself he was an eccentric foreign character, which must naturally be an interesting study for a stranger.

Presently the Princess took her to see the house. Every room was filled with relics. There were portraits of Peter the Great, and the splendid Catherine, in almost every room.

"The Empress was so much misjudged in your country, Tamara," her godmother said. "She had the soul and the necessities of a man, but she was truly great."

For luncheon quite a number of guests arrived; the Princess, she found afterwards, was hardly ever alone.

"I don't care to go out as a rule, to *dejeuner*," she said, "but I love my house to be filled with young people and mirth."

The names were very difficult for Tamara to catch, especially as they all called each other by their *petits noms*, all having been friends since babyhood, if not, as often was the case, related by ties of blood.

However she began to know that "Olga" was the Countess Gleboff, and "Sonia," the Princess Solentzeff-Zasiekin, both young, under thirty, and both attractive, and quite *sans gene*.

"Olga" was little, and plump, with an oval face and rather prominent eyes, but with a way of saying things which enchanted Tamara's ear.

They were all so amusing and gay at lunch. Quantities of pleasant things were planned, and Tamara found her days arranged for a week ahead.

That night, as they drove to Prince Milaslavski's dinner, an annoying sense of excitement possessed Tamara.

She refused to ask herself why it was.

Curiosity to see the house of this strange man, most likely; in any case, emotion enough to make her eyes bright.

It was one of the oldest houses in Petersburg, built in the time of Catherine, about 1769, and stood, except for a few Empire rooms, a monument of its time.

Everything about it interested Tamara. The strange Cossack servants in the hall; the splendid staircase of stone and marble; and then finally they reached the Salons above.

The guests were all assembled, but host there was not!

"What an impertinence to keep them waiting like this!" Tamara thought.

However, no one seemed to mind but herself, and they all stood laughing or sitting on the fender in the best of spirits.

"I will bet you," said Olga Gleboff, in her attractive voice, "that Gritzko comes in with no apology, and that we shall none of us be able to drag from him where he has been!"

As she spoke he entered the room.

"Ah! you are all very early," he said, shaking their hands in frank welcome. "So good of you, dear friends. Perhaps I am a little late, you will forgive me, I know."

The dining-room doors at the side opened

and they all went in *en bande,* and gathered round the high table, where they began to eat.

It was so joyous and so perfectly without ceremony. "Nothing could be more agreeable than this society," Tamara thought.

"You must taste some vodka, Madame," Prince Milaslavski said, pouring out a small glass at Tamara's side. "You will not like it, but it is Russian, and you must learn. See, I take some too and drink your health!"

Tamara bowed and sipped the stuff, which she found very nasty, with a whiff of ether in it. Then they all trooped to the large table in this huge dining-hall.

Tamara sat on her host's right hand, and Princess Sonia on his left.

Tonight his coat was brown and the under-dress black, it was quite as becoming as the others she had seen him in, with the strange felt and trimmings and the Eastern hang of it all.

His great dark grey-blue eyes blazed at Tamara now and then with a challenge in them she could hardly withstand.

"Now tell us, Gritzko, what did you do in Egypt this year?" Princess Sonia said.

"I was studying mummies and falling in love with the Sphinx," he answered. "And just at the end I had a most interesting kind of experience; I came upon what looked like a woman, but turned out to be a mummy and later froze into a block of ice!"

"Gritzko!" they called in chorus. "Can anyone invent such impossible stories as you!"

"I assure you I am speaking the truth. Is it not so, Madame?"

He looked at Tamara and smiled with fleeting merry mockery in his eyes.

"Madame has been in Egypt, she tells me, and should be able to vouch for my truth."

Tamara pulled herself together.

"I think the Sphinx must have cast a spell over you, Prince," she said, "so that you could not distinguish the real from the false. I saw no women who were mummies and then turned into ice."

Someone distracted Princess Sonia's attention for a moment, and the Prince whispered:

"One can melt ice!"

"To find a mummy?" Tamara asked with grave innocence. "That would be the inverse rotation."

"And lastly a woman, in one's arms," the Prince said.

Tamara turned to her neighbour and became engrossed in his conversation for the rest of the repast.

Prince Milaslavski gave Tamara his arm and they found coffee awaiting them in the Salon when they returned there, and at once the rubbers were made up.

With faces of grave pre-occupation they sat down to their game, leaving only the Prince, one lady, and Tamara unprovided for.

"Yes, I can play," she had said, when she was asked, "but I do it so badly; may I not watch you instead?"

The lady who made the third had not these ideas, and she sat down near a table ready to cut in.

Thus the host and his English guest were left practically alone.

"I did not mean you to play," he said. "I knew you couldn't, I arranged it like this."

"Why did you know I couldn't?" Tamara asked. "I am too stupid perhaps, you think?"

"Yes, too stupid and too sweet."

"I am neither stupid nor sweet!"

Her eyes flashed.

"Probably not, but you seem so to me. Now don't get angry at once, it makes our acquaintance so fatiguing, I have each time to be presented over again."

Then Tamara laughed.

"It really is all very funny."

"And how is the estimable Mrs Hardcastle?" he asked, when he had laughed too. "This is a safe subject and we can sit on the fender without your wanting to push me into the fire."

"I am not at all sure of that," answered Tamara.

She could not resist his charm, she could not continue quarrelling with him; somehow it seemed too difficult here in his own house, so she smiled as she went on:

"If you laugh at my Millicent, I shall get very angry indeed."

"Laugh at your Millicent! The idea is miles from my brain. Did not I tell you when I could find a wife like that I would marry? What more can I say?"

The Prince got up and lit a cigarette.

"You do not smoke either? What a little good prude!"

"I am not a prude!" Tamara's ire rose again. "I have tried often with my brother Tom, and it always makes me sick. I would be a fool, not a prude, to go on, would I not?"

"I am not forcing you to smoke. I like your pretty teeth best as they are!"

Rebellion shook Tamara. It was his attitude towards her, one of supreme unconcerned command, as if he had a perfect right to take his pleasure out of her conversation, and play upon her emotions, according to his mood.

She could have boxed his ears.

"How long ago is it since we danced in Egypt, a fortnight, or more? You move well, but you don't know anything about dancing."

Tamara did not speak.

"I wonder what this music we shall hear will say to you. Will it make the milk and water you call blood in your veins race? It will amuse me to see."

"I am not made for your amusement, Prince. How dare you always treat me as you do?"

Tamara drew herself up haughtily. "And if my veins contain milk and water, it is at least my own."

"You dared me once before, Madame," he said, smiling provokingly. "Do you think it is quite wise of you to try it again?"

"I do not care if it is wise or no. I hate you!" hissed Tamara.

Then his eyes blazed, as she had never seen them yet. He moved nearer to her, and spoke in a low concentrated voice.

"It is a challenge. Good. Now listen to what I say. In a little short time you shall love me.

That haughty little head shall lie here on my breast without a struggle, and I shall kiss your lips until you cannot breathe."

For the second time in her life Tamara went dead white. He saw her pale even to her lips.

But since the moment was not yet, and since his mood was not now to make her suffer, he bent over with contrition and asked her to forgive him in a tender voice.

"Madame, I am only joking, but I am a brute."

Tamara rose and walked to the bridge tables, furious with herself that he could have seen his power over her, even though it was only to cause rage.

He came up behind her and sat down and began to talk nicely again. About the sights to be seen in the capital, and the interesting museums and collections of pictures and arms.

Nothing could be more correct than his manner, and the bridge players who were within earshot smiled, while Countess Olga thought:

"Either Gritzko has just been making love to the Englishwoman, or he is immensely bored."

Chapter
Four

The company stopped their game about a quarter to twelve, and tables and champagne and glasses were brought in, and hand in hand they made a circle and drank in the New Year.

Tamara took care to stand by Princess Ardacheff, but her host looked at her as he raised his glass.

Then they descended to the hall and were wrapped in their furs again to go to the cafe where the Bohemians were to sing.

Tamara and the Princess were already in the latter's coupe when Prince Milaslavski called out:

"Tantine, take me too, I am slim and can sit between you, and I want to arrive soon, I have sent my motor on with Serge and Valonne."

And without waiting he got in.

They had to sit very close, and Tamara became incensed with herself, because in spite of all her late rage with the Prince, she experienced a sensation which was disturbing and unknown.

The magnetic personality of the man was so strong.

He bent and whispered something to the Princess, and then, as though sharing a secret, he leaned the other way, and whispered to Tamara too.

The words were nothing, only some ordinary nonsense, of which she took no heed. But as he spoke his lips touched her ear.

A wild thrill ran through her, she almost trembled, so violent was the emotion the little accidental caress caused. It was a feeling she had never experienced in the whole of her life before.

Why did he tease her so? Why did he always behave in this maddening manner, and choose moments when she was defenceless and could make no move?

Of one thing she was certain, if she should stay on in Russia she must come to some understanding with him, and prevent any more of these ways. They were insulting to her self-respect.

She shrank back in her corner and gave no reply.

"Are you angry with me?" he whispered. "It was the shaking of the automobile which caused me to come too near you. Forgive me, I will try not to sin again."

As he spoke he repeated his offence!

Tamara clasped her hands together, tightly, and answered in the coldest voice:

"I did not notice anything, Prince, it must be a guilty conscience which causes you to apologise."

"In that case then all is well!" he laughed softly.

The Princess now joined in the conversation.

"Gritzko, you must tell Mrs Loraine who these gipsies are, and what she will hear. She will think it otherwise so strange."

He turned to Tamara at once.

"They are a queer people who dwell in a clan. They sing like a fiend and one hates it or loves it, but it gets on the nerves. If a man should fancy one of them, he must pay the Chief not the girl.

"They are faithful and money won't tempt them away. But if the man makes them jealous, they run a knife into his back."

"It sounds exciting at all events," Tamara said.

"It is an acquired taste, and if you have a particularly sensitive ear the music will make you feel inclined to scream. It drives me mad."

"Gritzko," the Princess whispered to him. "You promise to be sage, dear boy, do you not? Sometimes you alarm me, when you go too far."

"*Tantine!*" and he kissed her hand. "Your words are law!"

"Alas! if that were only true," she said with a sigh.

"Tonight all shall be suited to the eleven thousand virgins!" he laughed. "Or shall I say suited to an English *grande dame*, which is the same!"

They had crossed the Neva by now, and presently arrived at a building with a gloomy-looking door, and so to a dingy hall, in which a few waiters were scurrying about.

They seemed to go through endless shabby

passages, until Tamara found herself seated on the middle sofa behind the long table, Count Gleboff was on her right, and the French Secretary, Count Valonne, her left.

Their host stood up, a brimming glass in his hand.

Then there filed in about twenty-five of the most unattractive animal-looking females, dressed in ordinary hideous clothes, who all took their seats on a row of chairs at the farther end.

They wore no national costume nor anything to attract the eye, but were simply garbed as concierges or shop-girls might have been. Some were old, grey-haired women, one had even a swollen face tied up in a black scarf!

How could it be possible that any one of these could be the "fancy" of a man!

They were followed by about ten dark, beetle-browed males, who carried guitars.

These were the famous Bohemians! Their appearance at all events was disillusioning enough. Tamara's disappointment was immense.

But presently when they began to sing she realised that there was something in their music, even though it was of an intense unrest.

It was of the most wild, a queer metallic sound, and the airs were full of unexpected harmonies and nerve-racking chords. It fired the senses, in spite of the hideous singers.

They all sat there with perfectly immovable faces and entirely still hands, singing without gesticulations what were evidently passionate love-songs.

Nothing could have been more incongruous or grotesque!

But the fascination of it grew and grew. Every one of their ugly faces remained printed on Tamara's brain. Long afterwards she would see them in dreams.

How little did she know of the force of sounds! How little she knew of the great currents which affect the world and human life!

The music of these gipsies was of the Devil, it seemed to her, and she was not surprised at the wild look in Prince Milaslavski's eyes.

She herself, well brought up, a conventionally crushed Englishwoman, felt a strange quickening of the pulse.

After an hour or so of this music, two of the younger Bohemian women began to dance, not in the least with the movements that had shocked Mrs Hardcastle in the Alexandrian troupe on the ship, but a foolish valsing, while the shoulders rose and fell and quivered like the flapping wings of some bird.

About three o'clock the entire troupe filed out of the room for refreshment and rest.

The atmosphere was thick with smoke, and heated to an incredible extent. Someone started to play the piano, and everyone began to dance a wild mazurka.

Tamara found herself clasped tightly in the arms of her Prince.

She did not know the steps, but they valsed to the tune, and all the time he was whispering mad things in Russian in her ear.

She could not correct him, because she did not know what they might mean.

"*Doushka*," he said at last. "So you are awake; so it is not milk and water after all in those pretty blue veins! God! I will teach you to live!"

And Tamara was not angry; she felt nothing except an unreasoning pleasure and exultation.

The amateur bandsman came to a stop, and another took his place; but the spell fortunately was broken, and she could pull herself together and return to saner ways.

"I am tired," she said, when the Prince would have gone on, "and I am almost faint for want of air."

He opened a window and left her for a moment in peace.

She danced again with the first man who asked her, going quickly from one to another so as to avoid having to be too often held by the Prince. But each time she felt his arm round her, back again would steal the delicious mad thrill.

"I hope you are amusing yourself, dear child," her godmother said. "This is a Russian scene; you would not see it in any other land."

And indeed Tamara was happy, in spite of her agitation and unrest.

When the gipsies returned, their music grew wilder than ever, and some of the solos seemed to touch responsive chords in Tamara's very bones.

The Prince sat next her on the sofa now, and every few moments he would bend over to take an almond, or light a cigarette, so that he touched her.

The same new and intoxicating sensation would steal through her, and she would draw her slender figure away and try to be stiff and severe, but with no effect.

It was long after five o'clock before it was

all done, and they began to wrap up and say "Good-night." And the troupe, bowing, went off to another engagement.

"They sing all night and sleep in the day," Count Gleboff told Tamara, as they descended the stairs. "At this time of the year they never see daylight, only sometimes the dawn."

"*Tantine*," said the Prince, "order your motor to go back. I sent for my troika, and it is here. We must show Madame Loraine what a sleigh feels like."

And the Princess agreed.

Oh! the pleasure Tamara found when presently they were flying over the snow, the side horses galloping with swift, sure feet.

Under the furs she and her godmother felt no cold, while Gritzko, this wild Prince, sat facing them, his splendid eyes ablaze.

Presently they stopped and looked out on the Gulf of Finland and a vast view. Above were countless stars and a young, rising moon.

Tamara felt she was a part of them.

* * *

Six days went past before Tamara again saw the Prince. Whether he was busy or kept away because he wished to, she did not know, but a piqued sensation gradually began to rise as she thought of him.

"I must arrange for you to go to Tsarskoi-Selo to see the ceremony of the Emperor blessing the waters on the sixth of our January, Tamara," her godmother said, a day or two after the Bohemian feast.

"I have seen it so often, and I do not wish to stand about in the cold, but Sonia's husband is one of the aides-de-camp, and, as you know, she lives at Tsarskoi. Olga is going out there, and will take you with her."

And Tamara had gladly acquiesced.

Tsarskoi-Selo, which they reached after half an hour's train, seemed such a quaint place. Like some summer resort made up of wooden villas, only now they were all covered with snow.

She and Countess Olga had gone together to Princess Sonia's house, and from there to the palace grounds.

The sky was heavy, and soon the snow began to fall intermittently in big, fluffy flakes. This background of white showed up the brilliant scarlet uniforms of the escort.

Suddenly Tamara saw the Prince. He was talking to some other officers, and apparently did not see them.

She grew angry with herself at finding how the very sight of him moved her.

The procession was as a lesser interest, her whole concentration being upon one scarlet form.

From the time the signal was given that the Emperor had started from the palace, all the heads were bare, in a temperature many degrees below freezing and in falling snow!

It was the Prince who gave the word of command, and while he stood at attention she watched his face. It was severe and rigid, like the face of a statue.

On duty he was evidently a different creature from the wild Gritzko of gipsy suppers. But there was no use arguing with herself, he attracted her in every case.

Then the procession advanced, and she

looked at it with growing amazement. This wonderful nation! so full of superstition and yet of common sense.

It seemed astonishing that grown-up people should seriously assist at this ceremony of sentiment.

When the Emperor passed she glanced again at the Prince. The setness of his face had given place to a look of devotion. There was evidently a great love for his master in his strange soul.

When the last figure had moved beyond the little temple corner, the tension of all was relaxed, and they stood at ease again, and Gritzko appeared to perceive the party of ladies, and smiled.

"I am coming to get some hot coffee after lunch, Sonia," he called out. "I promised Marie."

"Does it not give them cold?" Tamara asked, as she looked at the Cossacks' almost shaven bare heads. "And they have no great-coats on! What can they be made of, poor things?"

"They get accustomed to it, and it is not at all cold today, fortunately," Countess Olga said. "They would have their furs on if it were. Don't you think they are splendid men?

"I love to see them in their scarlet; they only wear it on special occasions and when they are with the Emperor, or at Court balls or birthdays. I am so glad you see Gritzko in his."

Tamara did not say she had already seen the Prince in the scarlet coat; none of her new friends were aware that they had met before in Egypt.

About ten minutes after they had finished lunch and were sitting at coffee in Princess

Sonia's cosy Salon, they heard a good deal of noise in the passage and the Prince came in.

He was followed by a sturdy boy of eight, and carried in his arms a tiny girl, whose poor small body looked wizened, while in her little arms she held a crutch.

"We met in the hall, my friend Marie and I," he said, as he bent to kiss Princess Sonia's hand, and then the other two ladies', "and we have a great deal to say to one another."

"These are my children, Mrs Loraine," Princess Sonia said. "They were coming down to see you; but now Gritzko has appeared we shall receive no attention, I fear."

She laughed happily, while the little boy came forward, and with beautiful manners kissed Tamara's hand.

"You are an English lady," he said, without the slightest accent. "Have you a little boy too?"

Tamara was obliged to own she had no children, which he seemed to think very unfortunate.

"Marie always has to have her own way, but while she is with Gritzko she is generally good," he announced.

"How splendidly you speak English!" Tamara said. "And only eight years old! I suppose you can talk French too as well as Russian?"

"Naturally, of course," he replied, with fine contempt. "But I'll tell you something, German I do very badly. We have a German governess, and I hate her. Her mouth is too full of teeth."

"That certainly is a disadvantage," Tamara agreed.

"When Gritzko gets up with us he makes her

in a fine rage! She spluttered so at him last week the bottom row fell out. We were glad!"

Princess Sonia now interrupted.

"What are you saying, Peter?" she said. "Poor *Fraulein!* You know I shall have to forbid Gritzko from going to tea with you. You are all so naughty when you get together!"

There was at once a fierce scream from the other side of the room.

"*Maman!* We will have Gritzko to tea! I love him! *Je l'aime!*" and the poor crippled tiny Marie nearly strangled her friend with a frantic embrace.

"You see, *Maman*, we defy you!" the Prince said, when he could speak.

The little boy now joined his sister, and both soon shrieked with laughter over some impossible tale which was being poured into their ears; and Princess Sonia said softly to Tamara:

"Gritzko is too wonderful with children, isn't he? All of ours simply adore him, and I can never tell you of his goodness and gentleness to Marie last year when she had her dreadful accident."

She sighed.

"The poor little one will be well someday, we hope, and so I do not allow myself now to be sad about it; but it was a terrible grief."

Tamara looked her sympathy, while she murmured a few words. Princess Sonia was such a sweet and charming lady.

Tamara was surprised at this new side of the Prince. It touched her. And he was such a gloriously good-looking picture as he sat there in his scarlet coat, while Marie played with the silver cartridges across his breast and Peter with his dagger.

When she and Countess Olga left to catch an early afternoon train he came too. He had to be back in Petersburg, he said.

When they got to the station the Princess's coupe was waiting, as well as the Gleboff sleigh.

"Good-bye, and a thousand thanks for taking me," Tamara said, and they waved as Countess Olga drove off.

And then the Prince handed her into the coupe and asked her if she would drop him on the way.

For some time after they were settled under the furs and rushing along, he seemed very silent, and when Tamara ventured a few remarks he answered mechanically.

"You are going to this bridge tournament at the Varishkine's, I suppose?" he suddenly said. "It ought to be just your affair."

"Why my affair?" Tamara asked, annoyed. "I hate bridge."

"So you do. I forgot. But *Tantine* will take you, all the same. Perhaps, if nothing more amusing turns up, I will drop in one night and see; but wheugh!"

He stretched himself and spread out his hands.

"I have been impossibly well behaved for over a fortnight. I believe I must soon break out."

"What does that mean, Prince, to 'break out'?"

"It means to throw off civilised things and be as mad as one is inclined."

63

He smiled mockingly while some queer, restless spirit dwelt in his eyes.

"I always break out when things make me think."

"That made you think?" asked Tamara, surprised.

"Never mind, good little angel. Good-bye."

He kissed her hand lightly and jumped out as they arrived at his house.

Tamara drove on to the Surguiefskaia with a great desire to see him again in her heart.

* * *

So the days passed and the hours flew. Tamara had been in Russia almost three weeks; and since the blessing of the waters the time had been taken up with a continual round of small entertainments.

The Court mourning prevented as yet any great balls; but there were receptions and "bridges" and dinners, and night after night they saw the same people, and Tamara got to know them well.

But after the excursion to Tsarskoi-Selo for several days she did not see the Prince. His military duties took up his whole time, her godmother said.

When at last he did come it was among a crowd, and there was no possible chance of speech.

"This bores me," he announced, when he found the room full of people.

He left in ten minutes, and they did not see him again for a week, when they met him at a dinner at the English Embassy.

Then he seemed cool and respectful and almost commonplace, and Tamara felt none of the satisfaction she should have done from this changed order of things.

It was late one afternoon, when Prince Milaslavski again came into view on Tamara's horizon.

She was sitting alone reading in the Blue Salon when he walked in.

"Give me some tea, Madame," he said. "The Princess met me in the hall, and told me I should find you here; so now let us begin by this."

Tamara poured it out. These two weeks, since the blessing of the waters, of unawakened emotions and just pleasant entertainments had given her a fresh poise.

"And what do you think of us by now, Madame?" he asked.

"I think you are a strange band," she said. "You are extremely intellectual, you are brilliant, and yet in five minutes all intelligence can fade out of your faces, and all interest from your talks, and you fly to bridge."

"It is because we are primitive and unspoilt; this is our new toy, and we must play with it; the excitement will wane, and a fresh one come."

He paused and went on in another tone:

"You in England have many outlets for your super-vitality."

"Have you ever been in England, Prince?" Tamara asked.

He sat down on the sofa beside her.

"No, but one day I shall go; Paris is as far as I have got on the road as yet."

"You would think us all very dull, I expect, calculating and restrained," Tamara said softly. "You might like the hunting, but somehow I do not see you in the picture there."

He got up and moved restlessly to the mantelpiece. There was almost an air of bravado in the insouciant tone of his next remark.

"Do you know, I did a dreadful thing," he said. "And it has grieved me terribly, and I must have your sympathy. I hurt my Arabian horse. You remember him, Suliman, at the Sphinx?"

"Yes," said Tamara.

"I had a little party to some of my friends, and we were rather gay, not a party you would have approved of, but one which pleased us all the same, and they dared me to ride Suliman from the stables to the big Salon."

"And I suppose you did?" Tamara's voice was full of contempt.

He noticed the tone, and went on defiantly:

"Of course; that was easy; only the devil of a carpet made him trip at the bottom again, and he has strained two of his beautiful feet. But you should have seen him!" he went on proudly. "As dainty as the finest gentleman in and out the chairs, and his great success was putting his forelegs on the fender seat!"

"How you have missed your metier!" Tamara said. "Think of the triumph you would have in a Hippodrome!"

He straightened himself suddenly, his great eyes flashed, and over his face came a fierceness she had not guessed.

"I thought you had melted a little, here in

our snow, but I see it is the mummy there all the same," he said.

Tamara laughed. For the first time it was she who held the reins.

"Even to the wrappings."

He took a step nearer her, and then he stood still, and while the fierceness remained in his face, his eyes were full of pain.

She glanced up at him, and over her came almost a sense of indignation that he should so unworthily pass his time.

"How you waste your life!" she said. "Oh! think to be a man, and free, and a great land-owner. To have thousands of peasants dependent upon one's frown. To have the opportunity of lifting them into something useful and good.

"Yet to spend one's hours and find one's pleasure in such things as this! Riding one's fav-ourite horse at the risk of its and one's own neck, up and down the stairs. I congratulate you, Prince!"

He drew himself up again, as if she had hit him, and the pain in his eyes turned to flame.

"I allow no one to criticise my conduct," he said. "If it amused me to ride a bear into this room and let it eat you up, I would not hesitate."

"I do not doubt it," and Tamara laughed scornfully. "It would be in a piece with all the rest."

He raised his head with an angry toss, and then they looked at each other like two fighting cats, when fortunately the door opened, and the Princess came in.

In a moment he laughed.

"Madame has been reading me a lecture," he said. "She thinks I am wasted in the Emperor's Escort, and a circus is my place."

Tamara did not speak.

"Why do you seem always to quarrel, Gritzko?" the Princess asked plaintively. "It really quite upsets me, dear boy."

"You must not worry, *Tantine*."

He kissed the Princess's hand.

"We don't quarrel; we are the best of friends; only we tell one another home truths. I came this afternoon to ask you if you will come to Milaslav next week.

"I think Madame ought to see Moscow, and we might make an excursion from there just for a night."

He looked at Tamara with a lifting of the brows.

"Then, *Tantine*, she could see how I cow my peasants with a knout, and grind them to starvation. It would be an interesting picture for her to take back to England."

"I should enjoy all that immensely, of course," Tamara said, pleasantly. "Many thanks, Prince."

"I shall be so honoured," and he bowed politely; then, turning to the Princess: "You will settle it, won't you, *Tantine?*"

"I will look at our engagements, dear boy. We will try to arrange it. I can tell you at the ballet."

The Princess smiled encouragingly up at him.

"My godchild has not seen our national dancing yet, so we go tonight with Prince Miklefski and Valonne."

"Then it is *au revoir*," he said, and kissing their hands he left them.

When the door was shut and they were alone:

"Tamara, what had you said to Gritzko to move him so?" the Princess asked. "I, who know every line of his face, tell you I have not seen him so moved since his mother's death."

So Tamara told her, describing the scene.

"My dear, you touched him in a tender spot," her godmother said. "His mother was a saint almost to those people at Milaslav; they worshipped her. She was very beautiful and very sweet, and after her husband's death she spent nearly all her life there.

"She started schools to teach the peasants useful things. She had such a tender heart, she longed to bring happiness to those in her keeping, and teach them to find happiness themselves."

"And he has let it all slide, I suppose," Tamara said.

"Well, not exactly that," and the Princess sighed deeply; "but I dare say these over-gay companions of his do not leave him much time for the arrangement such things require.

"Ah! If you knew, Tamara," she went on, "how fond I am of that boy, and how I feel the great and noble parts of his character are running to waste, you would understand my grief."

"You are so kind, dear *Marraine*," Tamara said. "But surely he must be very weak."

"No, he is not weak; it is a dare-devil wild strain in him that seems as if it must out. He has a will of iron, and never breaks his word!"

She sighed.

"Only to get him to be serious, or give his word, is as yet an unaccomplished task. I sometimes think if a great love could come into his life it would save him, his whole soul could wake."

Tamara looked down and clasped her hands.

"But it does not seem likely to happen, does it, *Marraine?*"

The Princess sighed again.

"I would like him to love you, dear child," she said.

Then as Tamara did not answer she went on softly almost to herself:

"My brother Alexis was just such another as Gritzko. That Season he spent with me in London, when your mother and I were young, he played all sorts of wild pranks. We three were always together. He was killed in a duel. It was all very sad."

Tamara stroked her godmother's hand.

"Dear, dear *Marraine,*" she said.

Then arm in arm they went to dress for dinner. They had grown real friends in these three short weeks.

Chapter
Five

The scene at the ballet was most brilliant, as it is always on a Sunday night.

The great auditorium, with its blue silk-curtained boxes, the mass of glittering uniforms, and the ladies in evening-dress, although they were all in black, made a gay spectacle almost like a gala night.

But Tamara, as she sat and looked at it, was not enjoying herself. She was overcome with a vague feeling of unrest.

She hated having to admit that the Prince was the cause of it. She could not look ahead; she was full of fear.

She knew now that when he was near her she experienced certain emotions, that he absorbed far too much of her thoughts. He did not really care for her probably, and if he did, how could one hope to be happy with such a wild, fierce man?

No, she must control herself; she must conquer his influence over her, and if she could not she could at least go away. England seemed very uninteresting, but calm and safe!

When the curtain went down, instead of the Prince joining them in the box, as she fully expected he would do, he calmly leaned against the orchestra division and surveyed the house with his glasses.

She felt a sudden pang, and talked as best she might to the many friends who thronged to pay the Princess court.

Gritzko did not even glance their way! He stood laughing with his comrades, and it would have been impossible to imagine anything more insouciant and attractive and provoking than the creature looked!

A wave of rage swept over her. She at least would not give in. *She would* be mistress of herself and her thoughts!

But alas! all these emotions, not unmixed with pique, spoilt the ballet's second act!

For the interval after it, the two ladies got up and went into the litle ante-chamber beyond the box. Tamara was glad. There she could not see what this annoying Prince would do.

What he did do was to open the door in a few minutes and saunter in. He greeted Tamara with polite indifference, and having calmly displaced Count Valonne, sat down by the Princess's side.

Valonne was a charming person, and he and Tamara were great friends. He chatted on now, and she smiled at him, but with ears preternaturally sharpened she heard the conversation of the other pair.

"*Tantine*, I am feeling the absolute devil to-night. Will you come and have supper with me after this infernal ballet is over?"

"Gritzko, what is it? Something has disturbed you?"

He leant forward and rested his chin on his hands.

"Well, your haughty guest touched me with too sharp a spur, perhaps, but she was right. I do waste my life. I have been thinking of my mother."

He paused.

"I believe she might not be pleased with me sometimes. Then I felt mad, and now I must do something to forget. So if you won't sup . . ."

"Oh! Gritzko!" the Princess said.

"I telephoned home and ordered things to be ready. I know you don't like a restaurant. Say you will come," and he kissed her hand. "I have asked all the rest."

"You must promise not to quarrel any more with my godchild if we do. I am sure you frighten and upset her, Gritzko, promise me."

He laughed.

"I upset her! She is too cold and good to be upset!"

Tamara still continued to talk to Valonne, and presently they all moved into the box, and the Prince sat down beside her.

As he leaned over in the shaded light, that nameless physical thrill crept over her.

"Am I really cold?" she asked herself.

If so, why should she shiver as she was shivering now?

"I wonder if you have any heart at all, Madame?" he said. "If under the mummy's wrappings there is some flesh and blood?"

She turned and answered him with passion.

"Of course there is."

He bent over still nearer.

"Just for tonight, shall we not quarrel or spar," he whispered. "See, I will treat you as a sister and friend. I want to be petted and spoilt, I am sad."

Tamara, of course, melted at once! His extraordinarily attractive voice was very deep and had a note in it which touched her heart.

"Please don't be sad," she said softly. "Perhaps you think I was unkind today, but indeed it was only because . . . oh! because it seemed to me such a waste that you should be like that."

"It hurt like the fiend, you know," he said, "the thought of the damned circus. I think we are particularly sensitive as a race to those sort of things. If you had been a man I would have killed you."

"I hated to hear what you told me. It seemed so dreadful, so barbaric, and so childish for a man who really has a brain.

"If you were just an animal person like some of the others are, it would not have mattered; but you, please, I would like you never to do any of these mad things again. . . ."

She stopped suddenly and grew tenderly pink. She realised the inference he must read in her words.

He did not speak for a moment, only devoured her with his great blue-grey eyes. Of what he was thinking she did not know.

It made her uncomfortable and a little

ashamed. Why had she melted? It was never any use. So she drew herself up stiffly and leaned back in her seat.

Then down at the side by the folds of her dress he caught her hand while he said quite low:

"Madame, I must know, do you mean that?"

"Yes," she said, and tried to take away her hand. "Yes, I mean that I think it dreadful for any human being to throw things away, and I would like you to be very great."

He did not let go her hand, indeed he held it the more tightly.

"You are a dear after all, and I will try," he said. "And when I have pleased you, you must give me a reward."

"Alas! What reward could I give you, Prince?" she sighed.

"That I will tell you when the time comes."

Peace seemed to be restored, and soon the curtain fell for the interval before the last act, and the Prince got up and went out of the box.

He did not reappear again, but was waiting for them to start for his house.

"I met Stephen Strong, *Tantine*," he said. "He left me at Trieste, you know, and only arrived in Petersburg today. He has got a cousin with him, Lord something, so I have asked them both to come along."

"It is not Jack Courtray by chance, is it?" Tamara asked, in an interested voice, as they went. "Mr Strong has a cousin who lives near us in the country and he is always travelling about."

"Yes, I think that is the name, Courtray. So you know him then!"

The Prince leaned forward from the seat which faced them.

"An *ami d'enfance?*"

"We used to play cricket and fish and bird's-nest," she said. "Tom, my brother, was his fag at Eton and he is one of my oldest friends. Dear old Jack."

"How fortunate I met him tonight!"

"Indeed yes."

Supper could not be ready for half an hour, the Prince told them when they arrived at Fontonka House, and they soon paired off for bridge.

"I am going to show Mrs Loraine my pictures," the host said. "She admires our Catherine and Peter the Great."

And in the Salon where they all sat, he began pointing out this one and that, making comments in a distrait voice.

But when they came to the double doors at the end he opened them wide, and led Tamara into another great room.

"This is the ballroom," he said. "It is like all the ballrooms, so we shall not linger over it."

The Prince talked intelligently. He seemed to know of such things as pictures and understand their technique. And if he had been an elderly art critic he could not have been more aloof.

Presently Tamara noticed underneath the first picture there was hung a quaint sword. Something in its shape and workmanship attracted her attention, and she asked its history.

The Prince took it down and placed it in her hand.

"That sword belonged to a famous person," he said. "A Cossack, Stenko Razin was his name, a robber and a brigand and a great Chief. He loved a Persian Princess whom he had captured.

"One day when out on his yacht on the Volga, being drunk from a present of brandy some Dutch travellers had brought him, he clasped her in his arms.

"She was very beautiful and gentle and full of exquisite caresses, and he loved her more than all his wealth.

"But mad thoughts mounted to his brain, and after making an oration to the Volga for all the riches and plunder she had brought him, he reproached himself that he had never given this river anything really valuable in return.

"Then exclaiming he would repair his fault, he unclasped the clinging arms of his mistress and flung her overboard."

"What a horrible brute!" exclaimed Tamara, and she put down the sword.

The Prince took it up and drew it from its sheath.

"The Cossacks had a wild strain in them even in those days," he said. "You must not be too hard on me for merely riding my horse!"

"Would you be cruel like that too? Tamara asked.

"Yes, I could be cruel, I expect," he said. "I could be even brutal if I were jealous, or the woman I loved played me false, but I would not be cruel to her while it hurt myself.

"Razin lost his pleasure through one mad personal act. It would have been more sensible to have kept her until he was tired of her, or she had grown cold to him. Don't you agree with me about that?"

"It is a horrible history and I hate it," Tamara said. "Such ways I do not understand. For me love means something tender and true which could never want to injure the thing it loved."

He looked at her gravely.

"Lately I have wondered what love could mean for me. Tell me what you think, Madame," he said.

She resolved not to, allow any emotion to master her, though she was conscious of a sudden beating of her heart.

"You would torture sometimes, and then you would caress."

"I would certainly caress."

He moved from his position and walked across the room, while he talked as if the words burst from him.

"Yes, I should demand unquestioning surrender, and if it were refused me, then I might be cruel. And if my love were cold or capricious, *then* I would leave her. But if she loved me truly, my God, it would be bliss."

"Think how it would hurt her when you did those foolish things though," Tamara said.

He stopped short in his restless walk.

"No one does foolish things when he is happy, Madame. All such outbursts are the froth of a soul in its seething. But if one were satisfied . . ."

He paused.

"Oh! If you knew! In the desert in Egypt I used to think I had found rest, sometimes. I am sated with this life here. I have wondered if perhaps you in your country could teach me peace."

"So many of you are so unbalanced," Tamara said. "You seem to be polished, sensible, and even great. Then in a moment you are off at a tangent, displaying that want of discipline that we at home would not permit in a child."

"Yes, it is true."

"It seems that you love, or you hate and must kill. There are storms, passions, and the gaiety of children, and on the top is good manners and smiles, but underneath I have a feeling a volcano may burst."

"Tonight I feel one could enflame in me."

He came up close now and looked into her eyes, as if he were going to say something, and then he restrained himself.

Tamara did not move, she looked at him gravely.

"You seem as if you had no aim," she said. "You are not interested in the politics of your country. You don't seem to do anything but kill time. Why?"

"Our country!" he said, and he flung himself into a seat near. "It would be difficult to make you understand about that. In the old days of the serfs, one could be a good landlord and father to them all, but now . . ."

He got up restlessly and paced the room.

"Now there are so many questions. If one would think it would drive one mad, but I am a soldier, Madame, so I do not permit myself to speculate at all."

"Things are not, then, as you would wish?" she asked.

"As I would wish? No, not as I would wish, but as I told you, I do not mix myself up with them. I only obey the Emperor and shall to the end of my life."

Tamara saw she had stirred too-deep waters. His face wore a look of profound melancholy. She had never felt so drawn towards him. She let her eyes take in the picture he made.

There was something very noble about his brow and the set of his head. Who could tell what thoughts were working in his brain?

Presently he got up again and knelt by her side. His movements had the grace and agility of a cat. He took her hand and kissed it.

"Madame, please don't make me think," he said. "For me, my only duty is my master. Nothing else could count."

His eyes, which looked into hers, seemed great sombre pools of unrest and pain.

She did not take away her hand, and he kissed it again.

Then the clock on the mantelpiece chimed one, and she started to her feet.

"Oh! Prince, should we not be thinking of supper?" she said. "Come, let us forget we have been serious and go back and eat!"

He rose.

"They have probably gone in without us, they know me so well," he said; "but as you say, we will not be serious, we will laugh."

Then he took her hand, and merrily, like two children, they ran through all the big empty rooms to find that exactly what he had predicted had occurred.

The party were at supper and quite unconcerned by their absence.

"Gritzko, we could not wait!" Countess Olga said.

Then both the Englishmen got up and greeted Tamara.

"Fancy seeing you here, Tamara! What a bit of luck!" Lord Courtray said.

Jack Courtray was a thoroughly good all-round sportsman, and as a rule had an immense success with women.

"This is a jolly place," Jack Courtray remarked.

Tamara, after the storms and emotions of the past few days, found a distinct pleasure and rest in his obviousness.

When all had finished supper, they moved back into another great room.

"You must notice this, Tamara, it is very Russian," her godmother said.

It was an immense apartment with a great porcelain stove at one corner, and panelled with wood, and it suggested to Tamara something of an orthodox church!

One end was bare, and the other carpeted with great Persian rugs, had huge divans spread about; there was an electric piano and an organ, and there were also crossed foils, and masks, and everything for a fencing bout.

The Prince went to the piano and started a valse. Then he came up to Tamara and asked her to dance.

There was no trace left of his respectful friendliness. His sleepy eyes were blazing, he had never looked more Oriental, or more savage, or more intense.

It was almost with a thrill of fear that Tamara yielded herself to his request.

He clasped her so tightly she could hardly breathe, all she knew was she seemed to be floating in the air, and to be crushed against his breast.

"Prince, please, I am suffocating!" she cried at last.

Then he swung her off her feet, and stopped by an armchair, and Tamara subsided into it, panting, not able to speak.

All across her milk-white chest there was now a row of red marks from the heavy silver cartridges, which cross in two rows in the Cossack dress.

"I would like those brands of me to last forever," the Prince said.

Tamara lay back in the chair, a prey to tumultuous emotions. She ought to be disgusted, she supposed, and of course she was.

But at the same time every nerve was tingling and her pulse was beating with the strange thrills she had only lately begun to dream about.

"Tamara! By Jove! What have you done to your neck?" Jack Courtray said, as he came up.

And Tamara was glad she had a gauze scarf over her arm, which she wrapped round carelessly as she said:

"Nothing, Jack . . . let's dance!"

"What an awfully decent chap our host is, isn't he?" Lord Courtray said, as they ambled along in their valse. "And jolly good-looking too, for a foreigner."

"Yes, he is good-looking," admitted Tamara.

"If he weren't so wild; but don't you think he has a frightfully savage expression, Jack?"

"If you are intending to play with him, old girl, take my advice, look out."

Meanwhile the Prince had left the room.

"Gritzko has gone to telephone for a Tzigane band," Princess Sonia said. "And to friends, to the club, and to the reception at Madame Sueboff's. Soon we shall have enough people for a *contre-danse*, and some real fun."

That it was almost three o'clock in the morning never seemed to have struck anyone!

"Now, tell me everything, Tamara," Lord Courtray said, as they sat down on one of the big divans.

"They are the nicest people you could possibly meet, Jack," Tamara said. "And don't imagine because they skylark like this, and sit up all night, that they aren't most dignified when they have to be.

"That is their charm, this sense of the fitness of things. They have not got to have any pretence like some of us have. Not one of them has a scrap of pose.

"They are nice because they like you, or they leave you entirely alone if they do not."

"And the men? I suppose they make awful love?"

"I don't think so," went on Tamara, while she stupidly blushed. "They all seem to be just merry friends, and the young ones don't go out very much.

"My godmother says they are very hard worked, and in their leisure they like to have dinners in their regiments.

"Or at restaurants with other sort of ladies, where they can do what they please. It seems a little elementary, don't you think so?"

"Jolly common sense!" said Jack Courtray.

Just then the Prince came into the room again, and the two men went off together to examine the foils.

Presently the band arrived and more guests, and soon the *contre-danse* was begun. That grown-up people could seriously take pleasure in this amazing romp was a new and delightful idea to Tamara.

It was a sort of enormous quadrille with numerous figures and farandole, while one sat on a chair between the figures, as at a cotillion.

Towards the end, the company stamped and cried, and the band sang, and nothing could have been more gay and exciting and wild.

Before they began, the Prince came up to Tamara and said:

"I want you to dance this with me. I have had it on purpose to show you a real Russian sight."

They had moved into the ballroom by then, which was now a blaze of light, while as if by magic the coverings had been removed from the chairs.

The Prince exerted himself to amuse and please his partner, and did not again clasp her too tight, only whenever she had turns with her countryman, his eyes would flame, and he would immediately interrupt them and carry her off.

Tamara felt perfectly happy, she was no longer analysing and questioning, and she was no longer fighting against her inclination. She abandoned herself to the rushing steam of life.

It was about five o'clock when someone suggested that supper at the Islands was now the proper thing. On no occasion was there ever a halt for the consideration of ways and means.

They wanted some particular amusement and had it! Convention, from an English point of view, remained an unknown quantity. Now those who decided to continue the feasting all got into their waiting conveyances.

"I know you like the troika, Tamara," Princess Ardacheff said. "So you go with Olga and Gritzko and your friend, only be sure you wrap up your head."

And when they were all getting in, the Countess Gleboff said:

"It is so terribly cold tonight, Gritzko. I am going to sit with my back to the horses, so as not to get the wind in my face."

When they were tucked in under the furs this arrangement seemed to Jack Courtray one of real worth, for he instantly proceeded to take Countess Olga's hand.

He whispered that he was cold and she could not be so inhuman as to let a poor stranger freeze!

It seemed amusing to look from the windows of a private room, down upon a gay supping throng, in the general salle at the restaurant on the Islands, while Tziganes played and their supper was being prepared.

"Who would think it was five oclock in the morning! What a lesson for our rotten old County Council in London," Jack Courtray said. "By Jove! this is the place for me!"

He proceded to make violent love to Olga

Gleboff, to whose side he remained persistently glued.

Then the gayest repast began; nothing could have been more entertaining or full of wild fun; and yet no one overdid it, or was vulgar or coarse.

At the last moment, when they were all starting for home about seven o'clock, Countess Olga decided she could not face the cold of the open sleigh, and Lord Courtray and she got into her motor instead.

It was done so quickly, Tamara was already packed into the troika, and the outside steeds were prancing in their desire to be off.

"The horses won't stand," the Prince said, and he jumped in beside her and gave the order to go.

Tamara found herself alone with him flying over the snow under the stars.

There was a delicious feeling of excitement in her veins.

They neither of them spoke for a while, but the Prince drew nearer and yet nearer, and presently his arm slipped around her, and he folded her close.

"*Doushka*," he whispered. "I hate the Englishman, and life is so short. Let us taste it while we may."

Then he bent and kissed her lips!

Tamara struggled against the intense intoxicating emotion she was experiencing. What frightful tide was this which had swept into her well-ordered life!

She vainly put up her arms and tried to push him away, but with each sign of revolt he held her the tighter.

"Darling," he said softly in her ear. "My little white soul. Do not fight, it is perfectly useless, because I *will* do what I wish. See, I will be gentle, and just caress you, if you do not madden me by trying to resist!"

Then he gathered her right into his arms, and again bent and most tenderly kissed her.

All power of movement seemed to desert Tamara. She only knew that she was wildly happy, that this was heaven, and she would wish it never to end.

She ceased struggling and closed her eyes, then he whispered all sorts of cooing love words in Russian and French, and rubbed his velvet eyelids against her cheek, and every few seconds his lips would seek her lips.

At last, when they had crossed the Troitzka bridge, because dawn was breaking and they could be observed, he released her, and only held her hands under the furs.

But when they turned into the wise Surguiefskaia, which seemed deserted, he bent once more and this time with wildest passion he seemed to draw her very soul through her lips.

Then before she could speak, they drew up at the door, and he lifted her out.

"Good-night, Madame, sleep well," he said calmly.

But Tamara, trembling with mad emotion, rushed quickly to her room.

Chapter
Six

In life there comes sometimes a tidal wave in the ebb of which all old landmarks are washed out. And so it was with Tamara.

She lay back in her pillows and forced herself to face the position, and review what she had done, and what she must now do.

First of all, she loved Gritzko, that she could no longer deny.

Secondly, she was English, and could not let herself be kissed by a man whose habit it was to play with whom he chose, and then pass on.

She was free, and he was free; it followed that his caressing, divine as it had been, was an absolute insult.

If he wanted her so much he should have asked her to marry him. He had not done so, therefore the only thing which remained for her to do was to go away. The sooner the better.

Then even as she lay there, a thrill swept over her, as her thoughts went back to that last passionate kiss. And her slender hands clenched under the clothes.

"If he really loved me," she sighed, "I would face the uncertain happiness with him. I know now he causes me emotions of which I never dreamed and for which I would pay the price."

She sighed.

"But I have no single proof that he does really love me. He may be playing in the same way as he has done before."

And at this picture her pride rose in wild revolt.

Never, never! should he play with her again at least!

Then she thought of all her stupid ways. Perhaps if she had been different, not so hampered by prejudice, but natural like all these women here, perhaps she could have made him really love her.

This possibility, however, brought no comfort, only increased regret.

The first thing now to be done was to restrain herself in an iron control. To meet him casually. To announce to her godmother that she must go home, and as soon as the visit to Moscow should be over, she would return to England.

She must not be too sudden, he would think she was afraid. She would be just stiff and polite and serene, and show him he was a matter of indifference to her, and that she had no intention to be trifled with again!

At last, aching in mind and body, she lay still.

Meanwhile, below in the Blue Salon, the Princess Ardacheff was conversing with Stephen Strong.

"Yes, *mon ami*," she was saying. "You must come, we go in a week, the day after my ball, to show Tamara Moscow, and from there to spend a night at Milaslav.

"Olga and Sonia and her husband and the Englishman, and Serge Grekoff and Valonne are coming, and it will be quite amusing."

Stephen Strong smiled.

"Since it is your wish, dear Princess, of course I must come."

They were old and very intimate friends, these two, and with him the Princess was accustomed to talk over most of her plans.

"Vera, tell me the truth," he said. "How are things going? I confess last night gave me qualms."

The Princess gazed at him enquiringly.

"Why qualms?"

"You see, Gritzko is quite an exceptional person, he is no type of a Russian or any other nation that one can reckon with, he is himself, and he has the most attractive magnetic personality a man could have."

"Well then?"

"And if you knew the simple unsophisticated atmosphere in which your godchild has been brought up."

"Stephen, really." The Princess tapped her foot impatiently. "Please speak out. Say what you mean."

"She is no more fitted to cope with him than a baby, that is what I mean."

"But why should she cope with him? Are not men tiresome!"

The Princess sighed.

"Can't you see I want them to love one another? If she would not snub and resist him all would be well."

"It did not look much like resistance last night," said Stephen Strong. "And if Gritzko is only playing the fool, and means nothing serious, then I think it is a shame."

"You don't suggest, surely, that I should interfere with fate?"

"Only to the extent of not giving him unlimited opportunities. You remember that season in London, and your brother Alexis, and her mother, and what came of that!"

The Princess put her hands up with a sudden gesture and covered her eyes.

"Oh! Stephen! how cruel of you to bring it back to me," she said; "but this is quite different, they are free, and it is my dearest wish that Tamara and Gritzko should be united."

Then she continued in another tone.

"I think you are quite wrong in any case. My plan is to throw them together as much as possible. He will see her real worth and delicate sweetness, and they will get over their quarrelling. It is her reserve and resistance which drives him mad. Sometimes I do not know how he will act."

"No, one can never count upon how he will act!" and Stephen Strong smiled. "But since you are satisfied I will say no more, only between you don't break my gentle little countrywoman's heart."

"You hurt me very much, Stephen!" the Princess said. "You, of all people, who know the tie there is between Tamara and me. You to suggest even that I would aid in breaking her heart!"

"Dear Vera, forgive me," and he kissed her plump white hand. "I will suggest nothing, and will leave it all to you, but do not forget a man's passions, and Gritzko, as we know, is not made of snow!"

"You all misjudge him, my poor Gritzko," the Princess said, hardly mollified. "He has the noblest nature underneath."

It was late in the afternoon when Tamara appeared, to find a room full of guests having tea. Her mind was made up, and she had regained her calm.

She would use the whole of her intelligence and play the game. She would be completely at ease and indifferent to Gritzko and be incidentally as nice as possible to Jack.

"For," she had reasoned with herself sadly, "if he had loved me really he would never have behaved as he has done."

So when the Prince and Lord Courtray came in together presently, her greeting to both was naturalness itself, and she took Jack off to a distant sofa with friendly familiarity, and conversed with him upon their home affairs.

It was Lord Courtray's fashion, when talking to any woman, even his own mother, to lean over her with rather a devoted look.

Tamara glancing up caught sight of Prince Milaslavski's face. It wore an expression which almost filled her with fear.

Of all things she must provoke no quarrel between him and dear old Jack, who was quite blameless in the affair.

At the same time there was a consolation in the knowledge that she could make him feel.

She thought it wiser soon to rise and return to the general group, while Jack, on his own amusement bent, now took his leave.

She sat down by Stephen Strong; she was in a most gracious mood it seemed.

"You have heard of our excursion to Moscow, Mr Strong," she said. "The Princess says you must come too; I am looking forward to it immensely."

"We ought to have a most promising time in front of us," he replied. "It all should be as full of adventure as an egg is full of meat!"

"Gritzko," Princess Ardacheff said. "How many versts is it from Moscow to Milaslav?"

The Prince had been leaning on the mantelpiece without speaking for some moments, listening to Tamara's conversation, but now he joined in, and sinking into a chair beside her, answered:

"Thirty verts, *Tantine*, we shall go in troikas, but you must send your servants on the night before."

Then he turned to Tamara, who seemed wonderfully absorbed, almost whispering to Stephen Strong.

"Did you sleep well, Madame?" he asked.

There was an expression of mocking defiance in his glance, which angered Tamara. However, faithful to her resolutions, she kept herself calm.

"Never better, thank you, Prince. It was a

most interesting evening, and I am learning the customs of your country. The thing which strikes me most is your wonderful chivalry to women, especially strange women."

They looked into one another's eyes and measured swords, and if she had known it she had never so deeply attracted him before.

She had broached the subject of her return to England to her godmother, who had laughed the idea to scorn, but now she spoke to Gritzko as if it were an established fact.

"I go home from Moscow," she said.

"You find our country too cold?" he asked.

"It is too full of contrasts, freezing one moment and thawing the next."

"All the same, you will not go," and he leaned back in the chair with his provoking lazy smile.

"Indeed, I shall."

"We shall see. There are a number of things for you to learn yet."

"What things?"

The Prince lit a cigarette.

"The possibilities of the unknown fires you have lit," he said. "You remember the night at the Sphinx, when we said good-bye. I told you a proverb they have there about meeting before dawn, and not parting until dawn."

He paused and said positively:

"Well, that dawn has not arrived yet. And I have no intention, for the moment, that it shall arrive."

Tamara felt excited, but as ever his tone of complete omnipotence annoyed her. At the same time to see him sitting there, his eyes fixed with deep interest on her face, thrilled and exalted her.

She certainly loved him. It would be dreadfully difficult to say good-bye. But three words in his sentence stung her pride—"for the moment!"

Yes, there was always this hint of caprice. Always he gave her the sensation of instability, there was no way to hold him. She must ever guard her emotions and ever be ready to fence.

And now that she had taken a resolve to go home, to linger no more, she was free to tease him as much as she could. To feel that she could gave her a fillip, and added a fresh charm to her face.

"You think you can rule the whole world to your will, Prince," she said.

"I can rule the parts of it I want, as you will find," he retorted fiercely.

"How amusing it would be if you happened to be mistaken this time," she cooed.

Then she rapidly turned to the Princess Sonia, who had just come in, and they all talked of the great ball which was to take place in the house in a week. The first after the period of the deep mourning.

"We cannot yet wear colours, but whites and greys and mauves, and won't it be a relief from all this black," Princess Sonia said.

When they had all gone and Tamara was dressing for dinner, she felt decidedly less depressed. She had succeeded better than she had hoped.

She had contrived to outwit the Prince; when he had vainly shown his intention was to continue talking to her, she had turned from one to another, and finally sat down by a handsome Chevalier Garde.

In company she had a chance, but when they were alone! However, that was simple, because she must arrange that they should never be alone.

* * *

It was perhaps a fortunate thing that for three days after this the Prince was kept at his military duties at Tsarskoi-Selo, and could not come to Petersburg, for he was in a mood that could easily mean mischief.

Tamara also was inclined to take things in no docile spirit.

She felt very unhappy, underneath her gay exterior. It was not agreeable to her self-respect to realise she was fleeing from a place because she loved a man whose actions showed he did not entertain the same degree of feeling for her.

No amount of attention from any other quite salved that ever-constant inward hurt.

But with all her will, hardly for ten minutes at a time could she keep Gritzko from her thoughts. His influence over her was growing into an obsession.

She wondered why he did not come. She would not ask her godmother.

The three days passed in a feverish, gnawing unrest; and on the third evening they went to the ballet again.

Opposite them, in a box, a very dark young woman was seated. She had a hard determined face, and she was well dressed, and not too covered with jewels.

"That is a celebrated lady," Count Valonne said. "You must look at her, Madame Loraine, she was one of the best dancers at the ballet, and last year she tried to commit suicide in a charmingly dramatic way at one of Gritzko's parties.

"She was at the time perhaps his *chere amie,* one never knows, but anyway violently in love with him, she still is, for the matter of that.

"In the middle of rather a wild feast he was giving for her, she suddenly drank off some poison, after making the terrifying announcement of her intention!

"We were all petrified with horror, but he remained quite calm, and, seizing her, he poured a whole bottle of salad oil down her throat, and then sent for a doctor.

"Of course the poor lady recovered, and the romantic end was quite spoilt! She was perfectly furious, and married a rich slate merchant the week after.

"Wasn't it like Gritzko? He said the affair was vulgar, sent her a large diamond bracelet, and never spoke to her again!"

Tamara felt her cheeks burn, and her pride galled her more than ever.

So she and the ex-dancer were in the same boat? But she at least would not try to commit suicide and be restored by salad oil!

"How perfectly ridiculous!" she said, with rather a bitter little laugh. "What complete bathos!"

"It was unfortunate, was it not?" Valonne went on, and he glanced at Tamara sideways.

He guessed that she was interested in the

Prince; but Valonne was a charming creature with an understanding eye, and in their set was in great request.

He knew exactly the right thing to talk about to each different person, as a perfect diplomat should, and he was too tactful and sympathetic to tease poor Tamara.

On the contrary, he told her casually that Gritzko had been on some duty these three days, in case she did not know it.

From the beginning Tamara always had liked Valonne.

Then into the box came the same good-looking Chevalier Garde, Count Varishkine, whom she had talked to on the last occasion of Gritzko's visit, and the spirit of hurt pride caused her to be most gracious with him.

Meanwhile, the Princess Ardacheff watched her with a faint sensation of uneasiness, and at last whispered to Stephen Strong:

"Does not my godchild seem to be developing new characteristics, Stephen? She is so very stately and quiet; and yet tonight it would almost seem she is being flirtatious with Boris Varishkine. I trust we shall have no complications. What do you think?"

Mr Strong laughed.

"It will depend upon how much it angers Gritzko. It could come to mean anything, bloodshed, a scandal, or merely bringing things to a crisis between them. Let us hope for the latter."

"Indeed yes."

"You must remember, for an Englishwoman it would be very difficult to grasp all the possibilities in the character of Gritzko. We are not accustomed to these tempestuous headlong natures in our calm country."

"Fortunately Boris and Gritzko are very great friends."

"I never heard that the warmest friendship prevented jealousy between men," Stephen Strong said, a little cynically.

"I am delighted we are going to Moscow. There will be no Boris, and I shall arrange for my two children to be together as much as possible. I feel that is the surest way," the Princess answered.

After the ballet was over the party went on to supper at Cubat's in a private room, contrary to the Princess's custom.

But it was Stephen Strong's entertainment, and he had no house to invite them to.

As they passed down the passage to their Salon, the door of another opened as a waiter came out, and loud laughter and clatter of glass burst forth, and above the din one shrill girl's treble screamed:

"Gritzko! Oh, Gritzko!"

The food nearly choked Tamara when they reached their room, and supper began.

It was not, of course, a heinous crime for the Prince to be entertaining ladies of another world. But on the top of everything else it raised a wild revolt in her heart, and a raging disgust with herself.

Never, never should she unbend to him again. She *would not* love him.

Alas! for the impotency of human wills!

Only the demonstrations of love can be controlled, the emotion itself comes from heaven, or hell, and is omnipotent.

Poor Tamara might as well have determined to keep the sun from rising as to keep herself frrom loving Gritzko.

She was quite aware that men, even the nicest men, like Jack and her brother Tom, sometimes went out with women she would not care to know, but to have the fact brought to her observation disgusted her fine senses.

To realise that the man she loved was at the moment perhaps kissing some ordinary woman revolted and galled her immeasurably.

But if she had known it, this night, at least, the Prince was innocent.

He had strolled into that room with some brother officers, and was not the giver of the feast. And a few minutes after Mr. Strong's party had begun their repast he opened the door.

"May I come in, Stephen?" he asked. "I heard you were all here, Serge saw you. I have just arrived from Tsarskoi, and must eat."

And of course he was warmly welcomed and pressed to take a seat, while Valonne chaffed him in an undertone about the joys he had precipitately left.

Tamara's face was the picture of disdain. But the Prince sat beside her godmother, apparently unconcerned.

He did not trouble to address her specially, and before the end of supper, in spite of rage, disgust, anger, and shame, she was longing for him to talk to her.

The only consolation she had was once

when they went out, as she looked up sweetly at Count Varishkine she caught a fierce expression stealing over Gritzko's face.

So even though he did not love her really he could still feel jealous; that was something, at all events!

Thus in these paltry rages and irritations, these two human beings passed the next three days, when their real souls were capable of something great.

Prince Milaslavski, to everyone's surprise, appeared continuously.

Tamara and the Princess met him everywhere, and while the Princess did her best to throw them together, Tamara manoeuvred so that not once could he speak to her alone, while she was assiduously charming to everyone else.

Now it was old Prince Miklefski or Stephen Strong, Jack, and just often enough to give things a zest she was bewitching to the handsome Chevalier Garde.

And the strange, fierce light in Gritzko's eyes did not decrease.

The night before the Ardacheff ball they were going to a reception at one of the Embassies for a foreign King and Queen, who were paying a visit to the Court.

Tamara dressed with unusual care, and fastened her high tiara in her soft brown hair.

The Prince should see her especially attractive, she thought.

But when they arrived at the great house and walked among the brilliant throng no Prince was to be seen. It might be he had no intention to come.

101

Presently Tamara went off to the refreshment room with her friend Valonne.

The conversation turned to Gritzko with an easy swing.

He seemed on the brink of one of his maddest fits. Valonne had seen him in the club just before dinner.

"If you really go to England I think he will follow you, Madame," he said.

"How ridiculous!" and Tamara laughed. "How can it make a difference to him whether I go or no? We do not exist for one another."

"I should not be quite sure of that," he said. "If I might predict, I should say you will be lucky if you get away from here without being the cause of a duel of some sort."

"A duel!" Tamara was startled. "How dreadful, and how silly! But why? I thought duelling had quite gone out in all civilised countries; and in any case, why fight about me? And who should fight? Surely you are only teasing me, Count Valonne."

"Duels are real facts here, I am afraid," he said. "Gritzko has already engaged in two of them. He is not quarrelsome, but just never permits anyone to cross his wishes or interfere with his game."

"But what *is* his game? You speak as though it were some kind of cards or plot. What do you mean?"

Tamara, with heightened colour, lifted her head.

"The game of Gritzko?" Count Valonne laughed. "Frankly, I think he is very much in love with you, Madame. So by that you can guess what would be any man's game."

"You have a vivid imagination, and are talking perfect nonsense," Tamara laughed nervously. "I refuse to be the least upset by such ideas!"

At the moment up came Count Boris Varishkine, and after a while she went off with him to a sofa by the window, and was seated in deep converse when the Prince came in.

He looked at them for a second and then made straight for the Princess Ardacheff, who was just about to arrange her rubber of bridge.

"*Tantine*, I want to talk to you," he said.

And the Princess at once left the card room and returned with him. They found a quiet corner opposite Tamara and her Garde, and there sat down.

"*Tantine*, I brought you here to look over there. What does that mean?"

The Princess put up her glasses to gain time.

"Nothing, dear boy. Tamara is merely amusing herself like all the rest of us at a party. Are you jealous, Gritzko?" she asked.

He looked at her sharply, and for a moment unconsciously fingered the dagger in his belt.

"Yes, I believe I am jealous. I am not at all sure that I do not love your charming friend."

"Why don't you marry her then?" suggested the Princess.

"Perhaps I shall, if she does not drive me to doing something mad first. I don't know what I intend. It may be to go off to the Caucasus, or to stay and make her love me so deeply that she will forgive me, no matter what I do."

He paused a moment, and his great eyes filled with mist, and then the wild light grew.

"If ever she becomes my Princess, she shall be entirely for me. I will not let her have a look or thought for any other man. All must be mine, unshared, and then she shall be my Queen."

Princess Ardacheff leant back and looked at him. He was in his blue uniform with the scarlet underdress. Even she, an old woman and fond friend, could not help picturing the gorgeous joy such a fate would give, to have him for a lover!

To see his fierce, proud head bent in devotion, to feel his tender caress. Tamara must be an unutterable fool if she should hesitate.

But what she had said was not reassuring in its prospect of calm. She felt she must put in some small word of admonition.

"You will be careful, won't you, Gritzko?" she ventured to suggest. "Remember, Tamara is an Englishwoman, and not accustomed to your ways."

"It will depend upon herself," he said. "If she goes on teasing me I do not know what I shall do. If she does not . . ."

"You will be good?"

"Possibly. But one thing, *Tantine*. I will not be interfered with either by her friend the Englishman or Boris Varishkine."

At this moment Tamara looked up and caught the two pairs of eyes fixed upon her. And into her spirit flowed a devilment.

Duels! They were all nonsense. She should certainly play a little with her own friend.

In her whole life before she came to Russia

she had never been really flirtatious. She was in no way a coquette, rather a simple creature who recked little of men.

But the simplest woman develops feline qualities under certain provocation; and her pride was deeply hurt.

Count Boris Varishkine asked nothing better than to fall in with her views. He was, however, like most of his countrymen, sincere, and not merely passing the time.

Jack Courtray came up too, and joined them. Tamara scintillated and sparkled as she talked to them both in a way which surprised herself.

Presently the little group was joined by Stephen Strong.

"Isn't this an amusing party, Mrs Loraine?" he said.

"Yes," said Tamara. "And I am beginning to be able to place the members of the different countries. Don't you think the Russians look much like us, Mr Strong?"

"The Russians, dear lady? When you have travelled a little more you will see that term covers half the types of the earth, but I agree."

"What we see here in Petersburg are very much like us, a trifling difference in the way the eyes are set, and the way the hair is brushed; and, given the same uniforms, half these smart young men might be our English Guards."

"We do not resemble you in character, though," said Count Varishkine. "You can feel just what you like, or not at all, whereas we are storm-tossed, and have not yet learnt the arts of pretence."

"We're a deuced cold-blooded race, aren't we, Tamara?" Jack Courtray said, and he grinned his happy grin.

The little party looked so merry and content Princess Ardacheff hardly liked to disturb them, but was impelled to by a look in Gritzko's face.

"Tamara, dear," she said, as she joined them. "I am so very tired after last night, for once shall we go home reasonably early?"

And Tamara rose gladly to her feet.

"Of course, *Marraine*, I too am dropping with fatigue," she said.

The Prince spoke a few words to Stephen Strong, and Jack joined in; so that the three were a pace or so to one side, when the two ladies wished them good-night.

"Come and see me early tomorrow, Jack," Tamara said. "I want to show you Tom's letter from home."

She looked up with an alluring smile, feeling the Prince was watching her; then, turning to Count Boris:

"I am sure you will regret your bargain in having asked me to dance the mazurka tomorrow night," she said. "I do not know a single figure or a step, but I hope we shall have some fun. I am looking forward to it."

"More than fun!" the young man said, with devotion, as he kissed her hand.

Then they walked to say good-night to the hostess, and Gritzko seemed to disappear. But when they got down into the hall they saw him already in his furs.

The Princess's footman began to hand Tamara her snow-boots and cloak, but Gritzko almost snatched them from the man's hand.

She made no protests, but let him help her to put them on and wrap her up, while her godmother thought it advisable to walk towards the door.

"Tonight was your moment, Madame," he said, in a low voice. "But the gods are often kind to me, and my hour will come!"

Tamara summoned everything she knew of provokingness into her face as she looked up and answered:

"So be it, and good-night! *Monsieur le demon de Lermontoff!*"

Then she felt it prudent to run quickly after the Princess and get into the automobile!

Chapter
Seven

It was twenty-four hours later. The night of the Ardacheff ball had come. The glorious house made the background of a festive scene.

The company waited all round the galleries for the arrival of the Grand Dukes and the foreign King and Queen.

And Tamara stood by her godmother's side at the top of the stairs, a strange excitement flooding her veins.

Since the night before they had heard nothing of the Prince. And as each guest came in view, past the splendid footmen grouped like statues on every six steps, both women watched with quickening pulses for one insouciant Cossack face.

The Royalties arrived in a gorgeous train, and yet neither Gritzko nor Count Varishkine.

It might mean nothing, but it was curious all the same. The opening *contre-danse* was in full swing, and still they never came, and by the time of the second valse Tamara was a prey to a vague fear, while the Princess's uneasiness grew more than vague.

Tamara could not enjoy herself. She talked at random, she made her partners continually promenade through the Salons, and her eyes constantly scanned the doors.

She was valsing with Jack Courtray, and they stopped to look at the world.

"Are they not a wonderful people, Jack? Could anything be more decorous and dignified than they are tonight?

"And yet if you watch in the *contre-danse* their eyes have the same excited look as when we wildly capered after supper in Prince Milaslavski's house."

"Which reminds me, why is he not here?" asked Jack.

"I wish I knew," Tamara said. "Jack, be a dear and go and forage about and get hold of Serge Grekoff, if you can see him, or Mr Strong or Sasha Basmanoff, or someone who might know. But it seems as if none of them are here."

"As interested as that?" Lord Courtray laughed. "Well, my child, I'll do my best."

He relinquished her for the next turn and left her with Valonne, who had just arrived.

"Apparently I shall have to go partnerless for the mazurka," Tamara carelessly said while she watched the Frenchman's face with the corner of her eye. "I was engaged for it to Count Varishkine, and he has never turned up. I do wonder what has happened to him. Do you know?"

"I told you you would be lucky if you got away from here without some row of sorts, Madame," and Valonne smiled enigmatically.

"What do you mean? Please tell me," and Tamara looked pale.

"I mean nothing; only I fancy you will only see one of them tonight; which it will be is still on the cards."

A cold, sick feeling came over Tamara.

"You are not insinuating that they have been fighting?" she asked, with a tremble in her voice which she could not control.

But Valonne reassured her.

"I am insinuating nothing," he said, with a calm smile. "Let us have one more turn before this charming valse stops."

And, limp and nerveless, Tamara allowed herself to be whirled round the room; nor could she get anything further out of Valonne.

When it was over she sought in vain for her godmother or Jack or Stephen Strong.

The Princess was engaged with the Royalties and could not be approached, and neither of the men were to be seen.

The next half hour was agony, in which, with a white face and fixed smile, Tamara played her part, and then just before the mazurka was going to begin Gritzko came in.

It seemed as if her knees gave way under her for a moment, and she sat down in a seat.

The relief was so great. Whatever had happened he at least was safe.

She watched him securing two chairs in the best place, and then he crossed over to where she sat by the door to the refreshment room.

"*Bon soir, Madame,*" he said. "Will you take me as a substitute for your partner, Count Varishkine?"

He bowed with a courtly grace which seemed suited to the scene.

"He is, I regret to say, slightly indisposed, and has asked me to crave your indulgence for him and let me fill his place."

For a moment Tamara hesitated; she seemed to have lost the power of speech; she felt she must control her anxiety and curiosity, so at last she answered gravely:

"I am so very sorry! I hope it is nothing serious. He is so charming, Count Varishkine."

"Nothing serious. Shall we take our places? I have two chairs there not far from Olga and your friend."

Tamara, now that the tension was over, almost thought she would refuse, but the great relief and joy she felt in his presence overcame her pride, and she meekly followed him across the room.

They passed the Princess on the way, and as she apparently gave some laughing reply to the Ambassador she was with, she hurriedly whispered in Tamara's ear:

"For the love of God! Be careful with Gritzko tonight, my child."

When they were seated waiting for the dance to begin, Tamara noticed that the Prince was very pale, and that his eyes, circled with blue shadows, seemed to flame.

The certainty grew upon her that some mysterious tragic thing had taken place; but, frightened by the Princess's words, she did not question him.

She hardly spoke, and he was silent too. It seemed as though now he had gained his end and

111

secured her as a partner it was all he meant to do.

Presently he turned to her and asked lazily:

"Have you been amused since the Moravian reception? How have you passed the time? I have been at Tsarskoi again, and could not come to see *Tantine*."

"We have been quite happy, thanks, Prince," Tamara said. "Jack Courtray and I have spent the day studying the lovely things in the Hermitage. We must see what we can before we both go home."

Gritzko looked at her.

"I like him, he is a good fellow, your friend." Then he added reflectively:

"But if he spends too much time with you I hope the bears will eat him!"

This charitable wish was delivered in a grave, quiet voice, as though it had been a blessing.

"How horrible you are!" Tamara flushed. "Jack to be eaten by bears! Poor dear old Jack! What has he done?"

"Nothing, I hope, as yet; but time will tell. Now we must begin to dance."

And they rose, called to the centre by the Master of the Ceremonies to assist in a figure.

While the Prince was doing his part she noticed his movements seemed languid and not full of his usual wild *entrain,* and her feeling of unease and dread of she knew not what increased.

Tamara was very popular, and was hardly left for a moment on her chair when the flower figures began, so their conversations were disjointed, and at last almost ceased.

Unconsciously a stiff silence grew up between

them, caused, if she had known it, on his side, by severe physical pain.

She was surprised that he handed all his flowers to her but did not ask her to dance, nor did he rise to seek any other woman.

He just sat still, though presently, when magnificent red roses were brought in in a huge trophy, and Serge Grekoff was seen advancing with a sheaf of them to claim Tamara, he suddenly asked her to have a turn, and got up to begin.

She placed her hand on his arm, and she noticed he drew in his breath sharply and winced in the slightest degree.

But when she asked him if something hurt him, and what it was, he only laughed and said he was well, and they must dance; so away they whirled.

A feverish anxiety and excitement convulsed Tamara. What in heaven's name had occurred?

When they had finished and were seated again she plucked up courage to ask him:

"Prince, I feel sure Count Varishkine is not really ill. Something has happened. Tell me what it is."

"I never intended you to dance the mazurka with him," was all Gritzko said.

"And how have you prevented it?" Tamara asked, and grew pale to her lips.

"What does it matter to you?" he said. "Are you nervous about Boris?"

And now he turned and fully looked at her, and she was deeply moved by the expression in his face.

He was suffering extremely, she could distinguish that, but underneath the pain there was a wild triumph too.

Her whole being was wrung. Love and fear and solicitude and, yes, rebellion also had its place. And at last she said:

"I am nervous, not for Count Varishkine, but for what you may have done."

He leant back and laughed with almost his old irresponsible mirth.

"I can take care of my own deeds, thanks, Madame,' he said.

And then anger rose in Tamara beyond sympathy for pain.

She sat silent, staring in front of her; the strain of the evening was beginning to tell.

She hardly knew what he said, or she said, until the mazurka was at an end; all the impression it left with her was one of tension and fear.

Then the polonaise formed, and they went in to supper.

Here they were soon seated next to their own special friends, and Gritzko seemed to throw off all restraint.

He drank a great deal, and then poured out a glass of brandy and mixed it with the champagne.

He had never been more brilliant, and kept the table in a roar.

But Tamara felt as though she were turned into stone.

And so the night wore on. It was now four o'clock in the morning. The company all went to the galleries again to watch the departure of the King and Queen.

And, leaning on the marble balustrade next to the Prince, Tamara suddenly noticed a thin crimson stream trickle from under his sleeve to his glove.

He saw it too, and with an impatient exclamation of annoyance he moved back and disappeared in the crowd.

The rest of the ball for Tamara was a ghastly blank, although they kept it up with immense spirit until very late.

She seemed unable to get near the Princess, she was always surrounded, and when at last she did come upon her in deep converse with Valone:

"Tamara, dear," she said, "you must be so dreadfully tired. Slip off to bed. They will go on until daylight."

There was something in her face which prevented any questions.

So, cold and sick with apprehension, poor Tamara crept to her room, and, dismissing her weary maid, sat and rocked herself over her fire.

What horrible thing had occurred?

What was the meaning of that thin stream of blood?

* * *

Tamara and her godmother did not meet until nearly lunch-time next day. A little before that meal the Princess came into her room. Tamara was still in bed, perfectly exhausted with the strain of the night.

The Princess wore an anxious look of care, as she walked from the window to the dressing-table and then back again.

Finally she sat down and took up a glove which was lying on a cushion near.

"Tamara, you saw I talked last night with

Valonne, and this morning I sent for Serge Gre-koff, but he would not come, so I got Valonne again."

She paused an instant.

"I was extremely worried last night about Gritzko. I dare say you were not to blame, dear, but . . ."

"Please tell me, *Marraine*."

"It appears, as far as I can gather, they all dined at Fontonka House; Boris Varishkine and Gritzko have always been great friends.

"At the end of dinner, Valonne imagines, be-cause no one is sure what took place between them at this stage, Gritzko, it is supposed, said to Boris in quite an amiable way that he did not wish him to dance the mazurka with you, but to relinquish his right in his favour."

She paused again, and Tamara's eyes fixed themselves in fascinated fear on her face.

The Princess, after smoothing out the glove in her hand with nervous energy, went on:

"They had all had quite enough champagne, of course, and apparently Boris refused, and sug-gested that they should toss up and whoever won the toss should have first shot in the dark."

"Yes," said Tamara faintly.

"You know, dear, our boys are often very wild, and they have a game they play when they are at the end of their tether for something to do when quartered in some hopeless outpost, a kind of blind-man's buff, only it is all in the dark.

"The blind man stands in the middle of the room and the rest clap hands, and then dodge and he fires his revolver at the point the sound

116

seems to come from, and the object is not to get shot.

"You may have noticed Sasha Basmanoff has no left thumb? He lost it last year on just such a night."

"Oh! *Marraine*, how dreadful!" Tamara said.

"It is perhaps not a very civilised game," the Princess continued, "but we are not discussing that, I am telling you what occurred. Well, from this point Valonne and the rest were eyewitnesses.

"Gritzko and Boris, still laughing in rather a strained way, said they had some slight difference of opinion to settle, and had decided to do it in the ballroom, in the dark.

"I won't go into details of how many steps to the right or left the impromptu seconds arranged.

"It was settled when Sasha at one end and Serge at the other should shut the doors they should both fire, and if in three times neither was shot, both should give up their claim."

"It is too horrible! and for such a trifle," Tamara said, clutching the bedclothes.

The Princess went on.

"Valonne said they were both hit in the first round, and all the company burst into the room. Nothing seemed very serious, and they laughed and shook hands.

"So Valonne left to be in time for the ball, but this morning, he told me, he found Boris Varishkine had had a shoulder wound which bled very badly and quite prevented his coming.

"Gritzko was shot through the flesh of the right arm, and as soon as they could bind it up decently, as you know, he came on."

117

Tamara's face was as white as her pillow. She clasped her hands with a movement of anguish.

"Oh, *Marraine*, I am too unhappy," she wailed. "Indeed, indeed, I did nothing to cause this. You heard me, I only said to Count Varishkine I was looking forward to the dance. He is impossible, Gritzko. Oh! let me go home!"

"Alas! my child, what would be the good of that? If you went off tonight instead of coming to Moscow, it might create a talk; what we want is to prevent a scandal, to hush everything up.

"None of these men will tell, and your name will not be dragged into it. And if we go on our trip amicably as was arranged it will discountenance rumour.

"Gritzko and Boris are quite friends again. And if anything about the shooting does leak out, if no one has further cause for connecting you with it, they will generally think it merely one of Gritzko's mad parties."

She sighed.

"For heaven's sake let it all blow over, and after Moscow and a reasonable time, not to appear too hurried, you shall go home."

"But meanwhile, how can I know that he won't shoot at Jack? or do some other awful thing! He does not love me really, *Marraine*.

"It is all out of pride and devilment because he wants to win and conquer me and add me to his scalps, and I won't be conquered. I tell you I won't!"

The Princess did not know what to say, she was not perfectly sure in her own mind as to Gritzko's feelings, and she was too thoroughly ac-

118

quainted with his ways to hazard any theory as to his possible acts.

She felt it might not be fair to assure her godchild that he truly loved her. She could only think of tiding over matters for the time being.

"Tamara, dearest, could you at least try to keep the peace on our trip?" she asked. "Be gentle with him, and do not excite him in any way."

Tamara buried her face in her pillows, she was too English to be dramatic and sob; but when she spoke her soft voice trembled a little and her eyes glistened with tears.

"He is horribly cruel, *Marraine*," she said. "Why should he treat me as he does? I can't . . . I won't bear it."

The Princess sighed.

"Tamara, forgive me for asking you, but I must, I feel I must. Do you love him, child?"

Then passion flamed up in Tamara's white face, her secret was her own, and she would defend it even from this kind friend.

"I believe I hate him!" she said.

After a while the Princess left her, they having come to the agreement that Tamara should do all that she could to keep the peace; but when she was alone she decided to speak to Gritzko as little as possible herself, and to ignore him completely.

There would be no Boris, and no one to make him jealous. She would occupy herself with Stephen Strong, and the sight-seeing.

She knew that she loved him deeply, this wild, fierce Gritzko, more deeply than ever today, and the tears, one after another, trickled down her pale cheeks.

Their train for Moscow started at nine o'clock, and the whole party had arranged to dine at the Ardacheff house at seven and then go to the station.

Nothing of the scandal of the night seemed to have transpired, for no one even hinted at anything about it.

Gritzko was still very pale, but appeared none the worse, and the atmosphere seemed to have resumed a peaceful note.

The five sleeping compartments, reserved for this party of ten, were all in a row in one carriage, and Tamara and the Princess, on the plea of fatigue, immediately retired to their berths for the night, Tamara not having addressed a single direct word to Gritzko.

So far, so well. But when she was comfortably tucked into the top berth, and an hour or so later was just falling off to sleep, he knocked at the door, and the Princess, believing it to be the ticket-collector, opened it, and he put his head in.

The shade was drawn over the lamp and the compartment was in a blue gloom. Tamara was startled by hearing her godmother say:

"Gritzko! What do you want, dear boy, disturbing us like this?"

"I came to ask you to tie up my arm," he said. "I was practising with a pistol yesterday, and it went off and the bullet grazed the skin, and the damned thing has begun bleeding again. I know you are a trained nurse, *Tantine*."

He now pulled back the shade and they saw he was standing there quite *sans gene* in the same kind of blue silk pyjamas Tamara remembered to have seen once before.

His eyes, far from being tragic or serious, had the naughtiest, most mischievous twinkle in them, while he whispered to the Princess and enlisted her sympathy for his pain.

"Gritzko, dearest child, but you are suffering! But let me see! Wait in the passage until I have put on my dressing-gown, and then come in."

Tamara now thought it prudent to crouch down in the clothes and pretend to be asleep, while the kind Princess got up and arranged herself.

Then with a gentle tap the poor wounded one came in.

Tamara was conscious that her godmother was murmuring horrified and affectionate solicitations, as she busily set to work.

She was also conscious that Gritzko was standing with his shoulder leant against her berth. He was so tall he could look at her, in spite of her retirement to the furthest side, and she was horribly conscious of the magnetic power exercised by his eyes.

She longed quite to open hers, she longed really to look. She felt so nervous she almost gave a silly little laugh, but her will won, and her long eyelashes remained resting on her cheek.

"You darling. You are doing it beautifully!" he presently said, and then more softly:

"I had no idea how pretty your friend is! and how soundly she sleeps! Do you think I might kiss her, *Tantine?* I have always wanted to, only she is of such a severity I have been too frightened. May I, *Tantine?*"

His voice sounded coaxing and sweet, and Tamara felt sure he was caressing the Princess's hair with his free hand, for that lady kept murmuring:

"Have done, Gritzko! How can I bind your arm if you conduct yourself so. Not a moment of stillness! Truly what a naughty child, keep still."

Then she spoke more severely to him in Russian, and he laughed while he answered.

Presently the bandage was done, and standing on tip-toe he looked full at Tamara.

"And you think I must not kiss her? Oh! you are a most cruel *Tantine!* She is sound asleep and would never know, and it would be just one of the things which could cool my fever and help my arm."

But the Princess interposed, sternly, and getting really annoyed with him, he was forced to go.

But first he kissed her hand and thanked her and purred affection and gratitude with his astonishing charm, and the Princess's voice grew more and more mollified as she said:

"There, there, what a boy! Gritzko, dear child, begone!"

And all this while, with her long eyelashes resting upon her cheek, Tamara apparently slept peacefully on.

But when the door was safely shut and bolted, the Princess addressed her.

"You are not really asleep, Tamara, I suppose," she said. "You have heard? Is he not difficult? What is one to do with him? I can never remain angry long.

"Those caresses! *Mon Dieu!* I wish you would love each other and marry and go and live at Milaslav, and then we others might have a little peace and calm!"

"Marry him," and Tamara raised herself in bed. "One might as well marry a panther in a jungle, it would be quite as safe!"

But the Princess shook her head.

"There you are altogether wrong," she replied. "Once there were no continuous obstacles to his will, he would be gentle and adoring, he would be as tender and thoughtful as he is to me when I am ill."

Then into Tamara's brain there rushed visions of the unutterable pleasure this tenderness would mean, and she said:

"Don't let us talk, I want to sleep, *Marraine*."

And in the morning they arrived at Moscow.

Chapter
Eight

The whole day of the sight-seeing passed with comparative smoothness, Tamara persistently remained with Stephen Strong, when any moment came that she should be alone with any man.

She was apparently indifferent to Gritzko, but she was throbbing with interest in his every movement. Inwardly longing to talk to him, she kept up the role she had set herself.

It was not an agreeable one, and but for the inward feverish excitement she would have suffered much pain.

Gritzko for his part seemed whimsically indifferent for most of the time, but once now and then the Princess, who watched things as the god in the car, experienced a sense of uneasiness.

And yet she could not suggest any other line of conduct for Tamara to pursue. But on the whole the day was a success.

The two young English guests had both been extremely interested in what they saw.

The snow fortunately had held, and they rushed about in little sleighs, seeing the quaint buildings and picturesque streets and the churches with their bright gilt domes.

Moscow was really Russian, Prince Solentzeff-Zasiekin told them; unlike Petersburg, which at a first glance might be Berlin or Vienna, or anywhere else; but Moscow is like no other city in the world.

"How extremely good you Russians must be," Tamara said. "The quantities of churches you have, and everywhere the people seem so devout. Look at them kissing that Ikon in the street! Such faith is beautiful to see."

They were waiting by the house of the Romanoffs, for their guide to open the door, and just then a batch of beggars passed, their wild hair and terribly ragged sheepskins making them a queer gruesome sight.

They craved alms with the same patient smile with which they thanked when money was given. Misery seemed to stalk about a good deal.

"How could a great family have lived in this tiny house?" Tamara asked. "Really people in olden times seem to have been able to double up anywhere. Pray, look at this bedroom and this ridiculous bed!"

"It will prepare you for what you are coming to at Milaslav," Gritzko said. "A row of tent stretchers for everyone together in the hall!"

Tamara made no answer, she contrived to move on directly he spoke, and her reply now was to the general company, as it had been all day.

If she had looked back then she would have seen a gleam in his eyes which boded no peace.

She thought she was doing everything for the best, but each rebuff was adding fuel to that wild fire in his blood.

By the end of the day, after walks through the Treasury and museums, and what not, and never having been able to speak to Tamara, his temper was at boiling-point.

But he controlled it, and his face wore a mask, which disarmed even the Princess's fears.

After dinner, Gritzko's eyes were blazing, and he suggested every sort of astonishing way to spend the night.

But Princess Ardacheff, as the doyenne of the party, prudently put her foot down, and insisted upon bed.

Had they not a whole morning of sight-seeing still to do on the morrow, and then their thirty versts in troikas to arrive at Milaslav. So the ladies all trooped off to rest.

"Leave your door open into my room, Tamara dear, if you do not mind," her godmother said. "I am always nervous in hotels.

"I trust everything is going quietly," she added to herself, "but one never can tell."

Next day the whole sky was leaden with unfallen snow. Nothing more strange and gloomy and barbaric than Moscow could have been imagined, Tamara thought.

It brought out the gilt domes and the unusual colours of things in a lurid way.

After an early lunch they saw from the hotel windows three troikas drawn up. Two of them Gritzko's, and one belonging to Prince Solentzeff -Zasiekin, who had also a country place in the neighbourhood.

126

The two, which had come a day or so before from Milaslav, were indeed wonderful turn-outs. The Prince prided himself upon his horses, which were renowned throughout Europe.

The graceful shaped sleighs, with the drivers in their quaint liveries standing up to drive, always unconsciously suggest that their origin must have been some chariot from Rome.

Gritzko's colours were a rich greenish blue, while the reins and velvet caps and belts of the drivers were a dull cerise.

The caps were braided with silver, while they and the coats and the blue velvet rugs were lined and bordered with sable.

One set of horses was coal black, and the others a dark grey. Everything seemed in keeping with the buildings, and the semi-Byzantine scene with its Oriental note of picturesque grace.

"Which will you choose to go in, Madame?" Gritzko asked. "Shall you be drawn by the blacks or the greys?"

"I would prefer the blacks," Tamara replied. "I always love black horses, and these are such beautiful ones."

"If you will come with Stephen and me, *Tantine*," the Prince said, "we shall be the lighter load and get there first.

"Madame Loraine and Olga can go with Serge and Lord Courtray, they will take the blacks; that leaves Valonne for Sonia and her husband. Will this please everyone?"

It was an enchanting drive over the snow. They seemed to fly along, once they had left the town, and the weird bleak country, unmarked by any boundaries, impressed both Tamara and Jack.

They at last skirted a dark forest, which seemed to stretch for miles, and then after nearly three hours' drive arrived at the entrance to Milaslav.

They went through a wild rough sort of park, and then came in view of the house, a great place with tall Ionic pillars supporting the front, and wings on each side, while beyond, stretching in an irregular mass, was a wooden structure of a much earlier date.

It all appeared delightfully incongruous and a trifle makeshift to Tamara and Jack, when they got out of their sleigh and were welcomed by their host.

A bare hall, at one side showing discoloured marks of mould on the wall, decorated in what was the Russian Empire style, a beautiful conception retaining the classic lines of the French and yet with an added richness of its own.

Then on up to a first floor, by wide stairs.

There were quantities of servants in their quaint liveries about, and when finally they arrived in a great Salon it was bright and warm, though there was no open fireplace, only the huge porcelain stove.

Some splendid skins of bears and wolves were on the floor, and there was a general air of the room being lived in, though magnificence and dilapidation mingled everywhere.

The very rich brocade on one of the sofas had the traces of great rents. And while one table held cigarette cases and cigar boxes in the most exquisitely fine enamel set with jewels, on another would be things of the roughest wood.

And a cabinet at the side, filled with a priceless collection of snuff boxes and *bonbonnieres* of Catherine's time, had the glass of one door cracked into a star of splinters.

Tamara had a sudden sensation of being a million miles away from England and her family; it all came as a breath of some other life.

She felt strangely nervous, she had not the least notion why. There was a reckless look about things which caused a weird thrill.

"If it were only arranged what capabilities it all has," she thought; "but as it is, it seems to speak of Gritzko and fierce strife."

Tamara wondered secretly what their sleeping accommodation would be like.

"*Tantine,* you must act hostess for me. Will you show these ladies their rooms," the Prince said. "Dinner is at eight o'clock, but you have lots of time before for a little bridge if you want."

He took them through the usual amount of reception rooms, a billiard room and library, and small boudoir, and then they came out to another staircase which led to the floor above.

Here he left them and returned to the men.

"This was done up by the late Princess, Tamara," her godmother said. "The whole house could be made beautiful if only there was someone who cared, though I expect we shall be comfortable enough."

Tamara's room and the Princess's joined. They were both gorgeously upholstered in crude blue satin brocade, and full of gilt heavy furniture, but in each there was a modern brass bed.

They were immense apartments, and warm and bright, monuments of the taste of 1878.

"Is it not incredible, *Marraine,* that with the

beautiful models of the eighteenth century in front of them, people could have perpetrated this. Waves of awful taste seem to come and artists lose their sense of beauty and produce the grotesque."

"This is a paradise compared to some," the Princess laughed. "You should see my sister-in-law's place!"

One bridge table was made up already when they got back to the Salon, and Sonia, Serge Grekoff, and Valonne only waited the Princess's advent to begin their game.

It seemed to be an understood thing that Gritzko and his English guest should be left out, and so practically alone.

"I feel it is my duty to learn to play better," Tamara said, "so I am going to watch."

He put down his hand and seized her wrist.

"You shall certainly not. You cannot be so rude as deliberately to controvert your host. It is my pleasure that you shall sit here and talk."

His eyes were flashing, and Tamara's spirit rose.

"What a savage you are, Prince," she laughed. "Everything must be only as you wish! That I want to watch the bridge does not enter into your consideration."

"Not a bit."

"Well, then, since I must stay here I shall be disagreeable and not say a word."

And she sat down primly and folded her hands.

He lit a cigarette, and she noticed his hand trembled a little, but his voice was quite steady, and in fact low as he said:

"I tell you frankly, if you go on treating me as you have done today, whatever happens is on your head."

"Do you mean to strangle me then? Or have me torn up by dogs?" Tamara smiled provokingly.

With all the others in the room, and almost within earshot, she felt perfectly safe.

She had suffered so much, it seemed good to oppose him a little, when it could not entail a duel with some unoffending man!

"I do not know yet what I shall be impelled to do, only I warn you, if you tease me, you will pay the price."

"He can do nothing tonight," Tamara thought, "and tomorrow we are going back to Moscow, and then I am returning home."

A spirit of devilment was in her. Nearly always it had been he who regulated things, and now it was her turn. She had been so very unhappy, and had only the outlook of dullness and regret.

Tonight she would retaliate, she would do as she felt inclined. So she leaned back in her chair and smiled, making a tantalising moue at him, while she said mockingly:

"Aren't you a barbarian, Prince! Only the days of Ivan the Terrible are over, thank goodness!"

He took a chair and sat down quietly, but the tone of his voice should have warned her as he said:

"You are counting upon the unknown."

She peeped at him now through half-closed alluring lids, and she noticed he was very pale.

In her quiet, well-ordered life she had never

come in contact with real passion. She had not the faintest idea of the vast depths she was stirring.

All she knew was she loved him very much, and the whole thing galled her pride horribly.

It seemed a satisfaction, a salve to her wounded vanity, to be able to make him feel, to punish him a little for all her pain.

"Think! This time next week I shall be safe in peaceful England, where we have not to combat the unknown."

"No?"

"No. *Marraine* and I have settled everything. I take the Wednesday's Nord Express after we get back to Petersburg."

"And tomorrow is Friday, and there are yet five days. Well, we must contrive to show you some more scenes of our uncivilised country, and perhaps after all you won't go."

Tamara laughed with gay scorn. She put out her little foot and tapped the edge of the great stove.

"For once I shall do as I please, Prince. I shall not ask your leave!"

His eyes seemed to gleam, and he lay perfectly still in his chair like some panther watching its prey.

Tamara's blood was up. She would not be dominated! She continued mocking and defying him until she drove him gradually mad.

But on one thing she had counted rightly, he could do nothing with them all in the room.

First one and then another left their game, and joined them for a few minutes, and then went back.

132

And so in this fashion the late afternoon passed and they went up to dress.

No one was down in the great Salon when Tamara and the Princess descended for dinner, but as they entered, Stephen Strong and Valonne came in from an opposite door and joined them near the stove, and Tamara and Valonne talked, while the other two wandered to a distant couch.

"Have you ever been to any of these wonderful parties one hears have taken place, Count Valonne?" she asked.

Valonne smiled his enigmatic smile.

"Yes," he said. "I have once or twice, perhaps you think this room shows traces of some rather violent amusements, and really, on looking round, I believe it does!"

Tamara shivered slightly. She had the feeling known as a goose walking over her grave.

"It is as if wild animals played here, hardly human beings," she said. "Look at that cabinet, and the sofa, that picture! One cannot help reflecting upon what caused those holes. One's imagination can conjure up extraordinary things."

"Not more extraordinary than the probable facts."

Valonne laughed as if at some astonishing recollection.

"You have not yet seen our host's own rooms though, I expect?"

"Why?" asked Tamara. "But can they possibly be worse than this?"

"No, that is just it. He had them done up by one of your English firms, and they are beautifully comfortable and correct.

"His sitting-room is full of books, and a few

good pictures, and leads into his bedroom and dressing-room; and as for the bathroom it is as perfect as any the best American plumber could invent!"

He laughed.

"He is the most remarkable contrast of wildness and civilisation I have ever met."

"It always seems to me as though he were trying to crush something, to banish something in himself," said Tamara. "As though he did these wild things to forget."

"It is the limitless nature warring against an impossible bar. If he were an Englishman he would soar to be one of the greatest of your country, Madame," Valonne said.

"You have not perhaps talked to him seriously; he is extraordinarily well read; and then on some point that we of the Occident have known as children, he will be completely ignorant, but he never bores one! Nothing he does makes one feel heavy like lead!"

Tamara looked so interested, Valonne went on.

"These servants down here absolutely idolise him; they have all been in the house since he or they were born. For them he can do no wrong.

"He has a gymnasium, and he keeps two or three of them to exercise him, and wrestle with him, and last year Basil, the second one, put his master's shoulder out of joint, and then tried to commit suicide with remorse. You can't, until you have been here a long time, understand their strange natures.

"So easily moved to passion, so fierce and barbaric, and yet so full of sentiment and fidelity.

I firmly believe if he were to order them to set fire to us all in our beds tonight, they would do it without a word!

"He is their personal 'Little Father.' For them there is a trinity to worship and respect, the Emperor, God, and their master!"

Tamara felt extremely moved. A passionate wild regret swept over her.

Oh! why might not fate let him love her really, so that they could be happy?

How she would adore to soothe him, and be tender and gentle and obedient, and bring him peace!

But just at that moment, with an air of exasperating insouciant insolence, he came into the room.

He began chafing with Valonne, and turning to her said something which set her wounded pride again all aflame, and burning with impotence and indignation she, as the strange guest, put her hand on his arm to go in to dinner.

Zacouska was partaken of, and then the serious repast began. Everyone was in the highest spirits. The whole party became worked up to a point of extra gaiety.

Gritzko sparkled with brilliancy and seemed to lead the entire table.

There was something so extremely attractive about him in his character of host that Tamara felt she dared hardly look at him or she could not possibly keep up this cold reserve if she did!

So she turned and talked, and apparently listened, with scarcely a pause, to her right-hand neighbour's endless dissertations upon Moscow.

While she answered interestedly, her

thoughts grew more and more full of rebellion and unrest.

It was as if a needle had an independent will, and yet was being drawn by a magnet against itself.

She had to use every bit of her force to keep her head turned to Prince Solentzeff-Zasiekin, and when Gritzko did address her, only to answer him in monosyllables, stiffly, but politely, as a stranger guest should.

By the end of dinner he was again wild with rage and exasperation.

When they got back to the great Salon, they found the end of it had been cleared and a semi-circle of chairs arranged for them to sit in and watch some performance.

It proved to be a troupe of Russian dancers and some Cossacks who made a remarkable display with swords, while musicians, in their national dress, accompanied the performance.

Gritzko's attitude towards them was that of the benevolent master to highly trained valued hounds. Indeed this feeling seemed to be mutual, the hounds adoring their master with blind devotion, as all his belongings did.

During most of the time he sat behind the Princess, and whispered whatever conversation he had in her ear; but every now and then he would move to Princess Sonia or Countess Olga, and lastly subsided close to Tamara, and bending over leaned on the back of her chair.

He did not speak, but his close proximity caused her to experience the exquisite physical thrill she feared and dreaded. When her heart beat like that, and her body tingled with sensation, it was almost impossible to keep her head.

His fierceness frightened her, but when he was gentle, she knew she melted at once, and only longed to be in his arms. So she drew herself up and shrank forward away from him, and began an excited conversation with Stephen Strong.

Gritzko got up abruptly and strode back to the Princess. And soon tables and supper were brought in, and there was a general move.

Tamara contrived to outwit him once more when he came up to speak. It was the only way, she felt. No half-measures would do now.

She loved him too much to be able to unbend an inch with safety. Otherwise it would be all over with her, and she could not resist.

They had been standing alone for an instant, and he said, looking passionately into her eyes:

"Tamara, do you know you are driving me crazy, do you think it wise?"

"I really don't care whether my conduct is wise or not, Prince," she replied. "As I told you, tonight, and from now onward, I shall do as I please."

She gathered all her forces together to put an indifferent look on her face.

"So be it then," he said, and turned instantly away, and for the rest of the time never addressed her again.

The long drive in the cold had made everyone sleepy, and contrary to their usual custom, they were all ready for bed soon after one o'clock, and to their great surprise Gritzko made no protest, but let the ladies quietly go.

Tamara's last thoughts before she closed her

weary eyes were, what a failure it all had been!
She had succeeded in nothing.

She loved him madly, and she was going
back home. And if she had made him suffer, it
was no consolation! She would much rather have
been happy in his arms!

Meanwhile, Gritzko had told Ivan, his Major-
domo, and ordered that early on the morrow the
stove was to be lit in the hut by the lake.

"And see that there is fodder for the horses,"
he added. "And that Stepan drives my troika
with the blacks, and let the brown team be ready
too, but neither of them to come round until the
greys have gone.

"And in the hut put food, cold food, and
some brandy and champagne."

The servant bowed in obedience and was
preparing to leave the room.

"Oil the locks and put the key in my overcoat pocket," his master called again.

Then he lit another cigarette and drawing
back the heavy curtains looked out on the night.

It was inky black, the snow had not yet begun to fall.

All promised well.

* * *

Tamara had just begun to dress when her
godmother came into her room next day.

"There is going to be a terrible snowstorm,
dear," she said. "I think we should get down fairly early and suggest to Gritzko that we start back
to Moscow before lunch. It is no joke to be caught
in this wild country."

"I won't be more than half an hour dressing,"

Tamara said. "Don't go down without me, *Marraine*."

The Princess promised and returned to her room.

"It has been a real success, our little outing, has it not?" she said, when later they were descending the stairs.

"Gritzko has been so quiet and nice. I am so happy, dear child, that you can go away now without that uncomfortable feeling of quarrelling.

"There was one moment when he got up from behind your chair last night and I feared you had angered him about something, but afterwards he was so gentle and charming when we talked I felt quite reassured."

"Yes, indeed," feebly responded Tamara.

The Princess beckoned to Gritzko and took him aside. She explained her fears about the storm, and the necessity of an earlier start, to which he agreed.

So it was arranged. The Princess and Stephen Strong were to start first, and Sonia and her husband would take both Serge and Valonne, leaving Gritzko to bring Tamara, Olga, and Lord Courtray last.

All through the early lunch, which was now brought in, nothing could have been more lamb-like than their host.

He exerted himself to be sweetly agreeable to everyone, and the Princess, generally so alert, felt tranquil and content, while Tamara almost experienced a sense of regret.

Only Count Valonne, if he had been asked,

would have suggested, but he was not officious and kept his ideas to himself.

The snow now began to fall, just a few thin flakes, but it made them hurry their departure.

In the general chatter and chaff no one noticed that Gritzko had never once spoken directly to Tamara, but she was conscious of it, and instead of its relieving her, she felt a sudden depression.

"You will be quite safe with Olga and your friend, dearest," the Princess whispered to her as she got into the first troika which came round. "And we shall be only just in front of you."

Then Princess Sonia's party started. The cold was intense, and as the team of blacks had not yet appeared, the host suggested the two ladies should go back and wait in the Salon.

"Don't you think our way of herding in parties here is quite ridiculous?" he said to Jack, when Olga and Tamara were gone.

"After the rest get some way on, I'll have round the brown team. It is going to be a frightful storm, and we shall go much better with only two in each sleigh."

Jack was entirely of his opinion; from his English point of view, a party of four made two of them superfluous. Countess Olga and himself were quite enough.

So he expressed his hearty approval of this arrangement, and presently as they smoked on the steps, the three brown horses trotted up.

"I'll go and fetch Olga," Gritzko said, and as luck would have it met her at the Salon door.

"I had forgotten my muff," she said, "and had just run up to fetch it."

Then he explained to her about the storm and the load, and since it was a question of duty to the poor horses, Countess Olga was delighted to let pleasure go with it hand in hand.

She allowed herself to be settled under the furs, with Jack, without going back to speak to Tamara. Indeed, Gritzko was so matter-of-fact she started without a qualm.

"We shall overtake you in ten minutes," he said. "The blacks are much the faster team."

And they gaily waved as they disappeared beyond the bend of the trees. Then he spoke to his faithful Ivan.

"In a quarter of an hour let the blacks come round."

And there was again the gleam of a panther in his eyes as he glanced at the snow.

All this while Tamara, seated by the Salon stove, was almost growing uneasy at being left so long alone. What could Olga be doing to stay such a time?

Then the door opened, and the Prince came in.

"We must start now," he said, in a coldly polite tone. "The storm is coming, and four persons made too heavy a load; so Lord Courtray and Olga have gone on."

Tamara's heart gave a great bound, but his face expressed nothing, and her sudden fear calmed.

He was ceremoniously polite as he helped her in. Nor did he sit too near her or change his manner one atom as they went along.

He hardly spoke; indeed they both had to crouch down in the furs to shelter from the blinding snow.

If Tamara had not been so preoccupied with keeping her woollen scarf tight over her head she would have noticed that when they left the park gate they turned to the right, in the full storm, not to the left, where it was clearer and which was the way they had come.

At last the Prince said something to the coachman in Russian, and the man shook his head, the going was terribly heavy. They seemed to be making tracks for themselves through untrodden snow.

"Stepan says we cannot possibly go much further, and we must shelter in the shooting hut," Gritzko announced gravely.

Again Tamara felt a twinge of fear.

"But what has become of the others?" she asked. "Why do we not see their tracks?"

"They are obliterated in five minutes. You do not understand the Russian storm," he said.

Tamara's heart now began to beat again rather wildly, but she reasoned with herself; she was no coward, and indeed why had she any cause for alarm?

No one could be more aloof than her companion seemed. She was already numb with cold too, and her common sense told her shelter of any sort would be acceptable.

They had turned into the forest by now, and the road, if road it could be called, was rather more distinct.

At last the view showed the white frozen lake, and by it a rough log hut. They came upon it suddenly, so that Tamara could only realise it was not large and rather low, when they drew up at the porch.

At the time she was too frozen and miserable to notice that the Prince unlocked the door, but afterwards she remembered she should have been struck by the strangeness of his having a key.

He helped her out, and she almost fell she was so stiff and cold, and then she found herself, after passing through a little passage, in a warm, large room.

It had a stove at one end, and the walls, distempered green, were hung with antlers.

There was one plain oak table and a bench behind it, a couple of wooden armchairs, a corner cupboard, and an immense couch with leather cushions, which evidently did for a bed, and on the floor were several wolf-skins.

The Prince made no explanation as to why there was a fire, he just helped Tamara off with her furs without a word; he hung them up on a peg and then divested himself of his own.

He wore a brown coat today, and was handsome as a god. Then, after he had examined the stove and looked from the window, he quietly left the room.

The contrast of the heat after the intense cold without made a tingling and singing in Tamara's ears. She was not sure, but thought she heard the key turn in the lock.

She started to her feet from the chair where she sat and rushed to try the door, and this time her heart again gave a terrible bound, and she stood sick with apprehension.

The door was bolted on the other side.

For a few awful moments which seemed an eternity, she was conscious of nothing but an agonised terror.

143

She could not reason or decide how to act. And then her fine courage came back, and she grew more calm.

She turned to the window, but that was double, and tightly shut and fastened up. There was no other exit, only this one door. Finding escape hopeless, she sat down and awaited the turn of events.

Perhaps he only meant to frightened her, perhaps there was some reason why the door must be barred; perhaps there were bears in this terribly lonely place.

She sat there reasoning with herself and controlling her nerves for moments which appeared like hours, and then she heard footsteps in the passage, breaking the awful silence, and the door opened, and Gritzko strode into the room.

He locked it after him, and pocketed the key; then he faced her. What she saw in his passionate eyes turned her lips grey with fear.

And now everything of that subtle thing in womankind which resists capture, came uppermost in Tamara's spirit. She loved him, but even so she would not be taken.

She stood holding on to the rough oak table like a deer at bay, her face deadly white, and her eyes wide and staring.

Then stealthily the Prince drew nearer, and with a spring seized her and clasped her in his arms.

"Now, now, you shall belong to me," he cried. "You are mine at last, and you shall pay for the hours of pain you have made me suffer!"

He rained mad kisses on her trembling lips.

A ghastly terror shook Tamara. This man

whom she loved, to whom she might have ceded all that he asked, now only filled her with frantic fear.

But she would not give in, she would rather die than be conquered.

"Gritzko, oh, Gritzko! please . . . please don't!" she cried, almost suffocated.

But she knew as she looked at him that he was beyond all hearing.

His splendid eyes blazed with the passion of a wild beast. She knew if she resisted him he would kill her. Well, better death than this hideous disgrace.

He held her from him for a second, and then lifted her in his arms.

But with the strength of terrified madness she grasped his wounded arm, and in the second in which he made a sudden wince, she gave an eel-like twist and slipped from his grasp.

As she did so she seized the pistol in his belt and stood erect while she placed the muzzle to her own white forehead.

"Touch me again, and I will shoot!" she gasped, and sank down on the bench almost exhausted behind the rough wooden table.

He made a step forward, but she lifted the pistol again to her head and leant her arm on the board to steady herself.

And thus they glared at each other, the hunter and the hunted.

"This is very clever of you, Madame," he said; "but do you think it will avail you anything? You can sit like that all night, if you wish, but before dawn I will take you."

Tamara did not answer.

Then he flung himself on the couch and lit a cigarette, and all that was savage and cruel in him flamed from his eyes.

"My God! what do you think it has been like since the beginning?" he said. "Your silly prudish fears and airs. And still I loved you, madly loved you.

"Since the night when I kissed your sweet lips you have made me go through hell, cold and provoking and disdainful.

"Last night when you defied me, then I determined you should belong to me by force; and now it is only a question of time.

"No power in heaven or earth can save you. If you had been different, how happy we might have been! But it is too late; the devil has won, and soon I will do what I please."

Tamara never stirred, and the strain of keeping the pistol to her head made her wrist ache.

For a long time there was silence, and the great heat caused a mist to swim before her eyes, and an overpowering drowsiness . . . Oh Heaven! . . . if unconsciousness should come upon her!

Then the daylight faded, and the Prince got up and lit a small oil lamp and set it on a shelf. He opened the stove and let the glow from the door flood the room.

Then he sat down again.

A benumbing agony crept over Tamara; her brain grew confused in the hot, airless room. It seemed as if everything swam round her. All she saw clearly were Gritzko's eyes.

There was a deathly silence, but for an occasional moan of wind in the pine trees. The drift

146

of snow without showed white as it gradually blocked the window.

Were they buried here, under the snow? Ah! she must fight against this horrible lethargy.

It was a strange picture. The rough hut room with its skins and antlers; the fair, civilised woman, delicate and dainty in her soft silk blouse, sitting there with the grim Cossack pistol at her head.

Opposite her, still as marble, the conquering savage man, handsome and splendid in his picturesque uniform; the dull glow of the stove, the one oil lamp, outside the moaning wind and the snow.

Presently Tamara's elbow slipped, and the pistol jerked forward.

In a second the Prince had sprung into an alert position, but she straightened herself, and put it back in its place, and he relaxed the tension, and once more reclined on the couch.

And now there floated through Tamara's confused brain the thought that perhaps it would be better to shoot in any case, and have done with it.

But the instinct of her youth stopped her, suicide was a sin, and while she did not reason, the habit of this belief kept its hold upon her.

So an hour passed in silence, then the agonising certainty came upon her that there must be an end. Her arm had grown numb.

Strange lights seemed to flash before her eyes. . . . Surely . . . that was Gritzko coming towards her . . . !

She gave a gasping cry and tried to pull the

trigger, but it was stiff, her fingers had gone to sleep and refused to obey her.

The pistol dropped from her nerveless grasp. So this was the end! He would win.

She gave one moan, and fell forward unconscious upon the table.

With a bound Gritzko leaped up, and seizing her in his arms carried her into the middle of the room.

Then he paused a moment to exult in his triumph.

Her little head, with its soft brown hair from which the fur cap had fallen, lay helpless on his breast.

The pathetic white face, with its childish curves and the long eyelashes resting on her cheek, made no movement. The faint, sweet scent of a great bunch of violets crushed in her belt came up to him.

Fiercely he bent to kiss her white, unconscious lips, suddenly he drew back, and all the savage exultation went out of him.

He gazed at her for a moment, and then carried her tenderly to the couch and laid her down. She never stirred. Was she dead? Oh, God!

In frightful anguish he put his ear to her heart; it did not seem to beat.

In wild fear he tore open her blouse, the better to listen. Yes, now he heard a faint sound. Saints in heaven! she was not dead.

Then he took off her boots to rub her cold little silk-stockinged feet, and her cold and damp hands. Presently as he watched, it seemed as if some colour came back to her cheeks, and at last she gave a sigh and moved her head without opening her eyes.

Then he saw that she was not unconscious now, but sleeping.

Then the bonds of all his mad passion burst, and as he knelt beside the couch, great tears suffused his eyes and trickled down his cheeks.

"My *doushka!* my love!" he whispered, brokenly. "Oh, God! and I would have hurt you!"

He rose quickly, and going to the window opened the ventilator at the top, picked up the pistol from the table and replaced it in his belt, and then he knelt once more beside Tamara, and with deepest reverence bent down and kissed her feet.

"Sleep, sleep, my sweet Princess," he said, softly, and then crept stealthily from the room.

Chapter Nine

The light was grey when Tamara awoke. Although the lamp still burned, more than three parts of the window was darkened by snow, only a peep of daylight flickered in at the top.

Where was she? What had happened? Something ghastly, but what?

Then she saw her torn blouse, and with a terrible pang remembrance came back to her.

She started up, and as she did so realised she was only in her stockinged feet.

For a moment she staggered a little and then fell back on the couch.

The awful certainty, or so it seemed to her, of what had occurred came upon her. Gritzko had won, she was utterly disgraced.

The whole training of her youth thundered at her. Of all sins, none had been thought so great as this which had happened to her.

She was an outcast. She, a proud English lady! She covered her face with her hands.

She moaned and rocked herself to and fro. Wild thoughts came, where was the pistol? She would end her life!

She looked everywhere, but it was gone.

Presently she crouched down in a corner like a cowed dog, too utterly overcome with shame and despair to move.

And there she still was when Gritzko entered the room.

She looked up at him piteously, and with unconscious instinct tried to pull together her torn blouse.

In a flash he saw what she thought, and one of those strange shades in his character made him come to a resolve.

Not until she should lie willingly in his arms, giving herself in love, would he tell her her belief was false!

He advanced up the room with a grave quiet face. His expression was inscrutable. She could read nothing from his look.

Her sick imagination told her he was thus serene because he had won, and she covered her face with her hands, while her cheeks flamed, and she sobbed.

Her weeping hurt him, he nearly relented, but as he came near she looked up.

No! Not in this mood would he win her! and his resolve held.

She did not make him any reproaches; she just sat there, a crumpled, pitiful figure in a corner on the floor.

"The snowstorm is over," he said in a restrained voice; "we can get on now. Some of my

Moujiks got here this morning, and I have been able to send word to the Princess that she should not be alarmed."

As Tamara did not move, he put out his hand and helped her up. She shuddered when he touched her, and her tears burst out afresh.

Where had all her pride gone? It lay trampled in the dust.

"You are tired and hungry, Madame," he said, "and here is a looking-glass and a comb and brush."

He opened a door of the tall cupboard which filled the corner opposite the stove, and took the things out for her.

"Perhaps you might like to arrange yourself while I bring you some food."

"How can I face the others, with this blouse!" she exclaimed miserably, and then her cheeks crimsoned again, and she looked down.

He did not make any explanation of how it had got torn, the moment was a wonderful one between them.

Over Tamara crept some strange emotion, and he walked to the door quickly to prevent himself from clasping her in his arms, and kissing away her fears.

When she was alone the cunning of all Eve's daughters filled her. Above all things she must now use her ingenuity to efface these startling proofs.

She darted to the cupboard and searched among the things there, and eventually found a rough housewife, and chose out a needle and coarse thread.

It was better than nothing, so she hurriedly drew off the blouse, then she saw her torn underthings, and another convulsive pang went through her, but she set to work.

She knew that however she might make even the blouse look to the casual eyes of her god-mother, she could never deceive her maid. Then the thought came that fortunately Johnson was in Petersburg, and all these things could be left behind at Moscow.

Yes, no one need ever know.

With feverish haste she cobbled up the holes, glancing nervously every few minutes to the door in case Gritzko should come in.

Then she put the garment on again, re-fastened her brooch, and brushed and recoiled her hair.

What she saw in the small looking-glass helped to restore her nerve. Except that her eyes were red, and she was very pale, she was tidy and properly clothed.

She sat down by the table and tried to think. These outside things could still look right, but nothing could restore her tarnished pride.

How could she ever take her blameless place in the world again?

Once more it hurt Gritzko terribly to see the woebegone, humbled, hopeless look on her face as he came in and put some food on the table.

He cut up some tempting bits and put them on her plate, while he told her she must eat, and she obeyed mechanically.

Then he poured out a tumbler of champagne, and made her drink it down. It revived her, and she said she was ready to start.

But as she stood he noticed that all her proud carriage of head was gone.

"My God! What should I feel like now," he said to himself, "if it were really true?"

He wrapped her in her furs with cold politeness, his manner had resumed the stiffness of their yesterday's drive.

Suddenly she felt it was not possible there could be this frightful secret between them. It must surely be all only a dreadful dream.

She began to speak, and he waited gravely for what she would say; but the words froze on her lips when she saw the pistol in his belt.

She shuddered convulsively and clenched her hands. He put on his furs quietly and then opened the door.

He lifted her into the troika which was waiting outside. Stepan's face, as he stood holding the reins, was as stolid as though nothing unusual had occured.

"I told the messenger to tell *Tantine* that we were caught in the snow," he said, "and had to take shelter at the farm.

"There is a farm a verst to the right after one passes the forest. It contains a comfortable farmer's wife and large family, and though you found it too confoundedly warm in their kitchen you passed a possible night."

"Very well," said Tamara with grim meekness.

Then there was silence.

Her thoughts became a little confused with the intense cold and the effect of the champagne, and once or twice she dozed off.

When he saw this he drew her close to him and let her sleep with her head against his arm, while he wrapped the furs round her so that she felt no cold. Then he kept watch over her tenderly, the fondest love in his eyes.

She would wake sometimes with a start and draw herself away, but soon fall off again, and in this fashion, neither speaking, the hours passed and they gradually drew near Moscow.

Then she woke completely with a shudder and sat up straight, and so they came to the hotel and found the Princess and the others anxiously waiting for them.

"What an unfortunate *contretemps*, Tamara, dear child," her godmother said, "that wicked storm! We only just arrived safely, and poor Olga and your friend fared no better than you!

"Imagine! They, too, had to take shelter in that second village in a most horrible hovel, which they shared with the cows. It has been too miserable for you all four I am afraid."

But Gritzko was obliged to turn quickly away to hide the irrepressible smile in his eyes. Really, sometimes fate seemed very kind.

So there was no scandal, only commiseration, and both Countess Olga and Tamara were petted and spoilt, while, if there was a roughish note in Valonne's sympathetic condolences, none of them appeared to notice it.

However, no petting seemed to revive Tamara.

"You have caught a thorough chill, I fear, dearest," the Princess said.

As they had missed their sleeping berths engaged for the night before, and were unable to get accommodation on the train again for the night, they were forced to remain in Moscow until the next day.

Therefore the Princess insisted upon her godchild going immediately to bed, while the rest of the party settled down to bridge.

"It is a jolly thing, a snowstorm!" Lord Courtray said to Gritzko.

But upstairs in the stiff hotel bedroom Tamara sobbed herself to sleep.

* * *

The journey back to Petersburg passed in a numb, hopeless dream for Tamara. She did her best to be natural and gay, but her white face, pinched and drawn, caused her godmother to feel anxious about her.

Gritzko had bidden them good-bye at the train, he was going back to Milaslav to arrange for his and Jack's bear-hunt, and would not be in the capital for two more days.

That would be the Tuesday, and Tamara was to leave on Wednesday evening by the Nord Express.

He had kissed her hand with respectful reverence as he said farewell, and the last she saw of him was standing there in his grey overcoat and high fur collar, a light in his eyes as they peered from beneath his Astrakhan cap.

They arrived late at night at the Ardacheff house, and the Princess sent for the doctor next day.

"Your friend has got a chill, and seems to have had a severe shock," he said when he came from Tamara's room. "Make her rest in bed today, and then distract her with cheerful society."

And the Princess pondered as she sat in the Blue Salon alone.

A shock . . . what had happened? Could fear

of the storm have caused a shock? She felt very worried.

And poor Tamara lay limp in her bed; but every now and then she would clench her hands in anguish as some fresh aspect of things struck her.

What if she should have ... ?

"No! Oh, no!" she unconsciously screamed aloud; and her godmother, coming into the room, was really alarmed.

From this moment onward the horror of this thought took root in her brain, and she knew no peace. But her will and her breeding came to her rescue.

She would not lie there like an invalid; she would get up and dress and go down to tea. She would chaff with the others, who would all swarm to see her.

No one should pity or speculate about her. Amidst the laughter and fun they had talking of their adventure, no one but Stephan Strong remarked on the feverish unrest in her eyes, or the bright, hectic flush in her cheeks.

When night came and she was alone again, her thoughts made a hell; she could not sleep; she paced her room.

If Gritzko should not return on Tuesday? If she should never see him again?

Next day, the Tuesday, at about eleven o'clock, a servant in the Milaslavski livery arrived with a letter, a stiff-looking large sealed letter.

She had never seen Gritzko's writing before and she looked at it critically as she tremblingly broke it open.

It was written from Milaslav the day they had left Moscow. It was short and to the point, and her eyes dilated as she read:

TO MADAME LORAINE,

MADAME, I write to ask you graciously to accord me the honour of your hand. If you will grant me this favour I will endeavour to make you happy. I have the honour, Madame, to remain,

Your humble and devoted serviteur,

GREGOIR MILASLAVSKI.

And as once before in her life Tamara's knees gave way under her, and she sat down hurriedly on the bed, all power of thought had left her.

"The messenger waits, ma'am," her maid said, stolidly, from the door.

Then she pulled herself together and went to the writing-table. Her hand trembled, but she steadied it, and wrote:

TO PRINCE MILASLAVSKI,

MONSIEUR, I have no choice. I consent,

Yours truly,

TAMARA LORAINE.

And she folded it, and placing it in the envelope, she sealed it with her own little monogram seal, in tender blue wax, and handed it to her maid, who left the room.

Then she stared in front of her, her arms crossed on the table, but she could not have analysed the emotions which were flooding her being.

Her godmother found her there still as an

image when presently she came to ask after her health.

"Tamara! dearest child. You worry me dreadfully. Confide in me, little one. Tell me what has happened?"

She placed her kind arms round her goddaughter's shoulders and caressed and comforted her.

Tamara shivered, and then stood up.

"I am going to marry Gritzko, *Marraine*," she said. "I have just sent him my answer."

And the Princess had too much tact to do more than embrace her, express her joy, and give her her blessing. All as if the news contained no flaw, and had come in the most delightful manner.

Then she left her alone in her room.

Yes, this was the only thing to be done, and the sooner the ceremony should be over the better.

Lent would come on in a few short weeks; that would be the excuse to hasten matters, and this idea was all Tamara was conscious of as she finished dressing.

At twelve o'clock, with formal ceremony, Prince Milaslavski sent to ask if the Princess Ardacheff could receive him. He was shown up into the first Salon, where the hostess awaited him.

He was dressed in his blue and scarlet uniform, and was groomed with even extra care, she noticed, as he advanced with none of his habitual easy familiarity to greet her.

"I come to ask your consent to my marriage with your goddaughter, *Tantine*," he said, with grave courtesy, as he kissed her hand. "She has

159

graciously promised to become my wife, and I have only to secure your consent to complete my felicity."

"Gritzko! my dear boy!" was all the Princess could murmur. "If you are sure it is for the happiness of you both, nothing of course could give me greater joy; but . . ."

"It will be for our happiness," he answered, letting the hinted doubt pass.

Then his ceremonious manner melted a little and he again kissed his old friend's hand.

"Dear *Tantine*, have no fears, I promise you it shall be for our happiness."

The Princess was deeply moved. She knew there must be something underneath all this, but she was accustomed to believe Gritzko blindly, and she felt that if he gave his word things might be right. She would ask no questions.

"Will you go and fetch my fiancée, like the darling you are," he said presently. "I want you to give her to me."

And the Princess, quite overcome with emotion, left the room.

It was not like a triumphant prospective Princess and bride that Tamara followed her godmother, when they returned together.

She looked a slender drooping girl, in a clinging dove-coloured gown, and she hardly raised her eyes from the carpet.

Her trembling hand was cold as death when the Princess took it and placed it in Gritzko's, and as they stood receiving her blessing she kissed them both, and then hurriedly made her exit.

When they were alone Tamara remained limp and still, her eyes fixed on the ground. It was he who broke the silence, as he took her left hand, and touched it with his lips.

He drew from her finger her wedding-ring and carelessly put it on a table. Then he placed his gift in the wedding-ring's place, a glittering thing of an immense diamond and ruby.

Tamara shivered.

She looked down at her hand, it seemed as if all safe and solid things were slipping from her with the removal of that plain gold band.

She made no remark as to the beauty of the token of her engagement, she did not thank him, she remained inert and nerveless.

"I thank you, Madame, for your consent," he said stiffly. "I will try to make you not regret it."

He used no word of love, nor did he attempt any caresses, although if she had looked up she would have seen the passionate tenderness brimming in his eyes, which he could not conceal.

But she did not raise her head, and it all seemed to her part of the same thing. He knew he had sinned against her, and was making the only reparation a gentleman could offer.

And even now with her hand in his, and the knowledge that soon she would be his Princess, there was no triumph or joy, only the sick sense of humiliation.

Passion, and its result, necessity, not love, had brought about this situation.

So she stood there in silence. It required the whole force of Gritzko's will to prevent him from folding her shrinking pitiful figure in his strong arms, and raining down kisses and love words upon her.

But the stubborn twist in his nature retained

its hold. No, that glorious moment should come with a blaze of sunlight when all was won, when he had made her love him in spite of everything.

Meanwhile, nothing but reserved homage, and a settling of details.

"You will let the marriage take place before Lent, won't you?" he said, dropping her hand.

And Tamara answered dully:

"I will marry you as soon as you wish," and she turned and sat down.

He leant on the mantelpiece and looked at her. He understood perfectly the reason which made her consent to any date, and he smiled with some strange powerful emotion, and yet his eye had a whimsical gleam.

"You are afraid that something can happen?" he said. "Well, I shall be most pleased when that day comes."

But poor Tamara could not bear this, the crystallising of her fears! With a stifled cry she buried her face in the cushions.

He did not attempt to comfort her, though he could hardly control his longing to do so.

Instead of which he said gravely:

"I suppose you must communicate with your family? They will come here perhaps for the wedding? Being a widow, you have not to ask any-one's consent by the laws of your country, have you?"

Tamara with a shamed crimson face half raised her head.

"I am free to do as I choose," she answered, and she looked down in crushed wretchedness. "Yes, I suppose they will come to the wedding."

"Lent is such an excellent excuse," he went

on. "And all this society is accustomed to my doing as I please, so there will be no great wonder over the haste. Only I am sorry if it inconveniences you, such hurried preparation."

"How long is it before Lent?" Tamara asked without interest.

"Just under a month, almost four weeks. Shall the wedding take place in about a fortnight? Then we can go south to the sun to spend our honeymoon."

"Just as you will," Tamara agreed in a deadly resigned voice.

"I am always confused by the difference between the English and the Russian dates. Will you write down what it will be that I may send it to my father?"

He picked up a calendar which lay upon the table, and made the calculations, then he jotted it all down on a card and handed it to her.

She took it, and, never looking at him, rose and made a step towards the door, and as she passed the table where he had put her wedding-ring she surreptitiously secured it.

"I suppose you are staying for lunch?" she said in the same monotonous voice. "Can I go now, do you want to say any more?"

"Tamara!" he exclaimed, with entreaty in his tone.

Then with quick repression he bowed gravely and once more touched her hand with his lips before he held open the door for her.

"I will be here when you return, I will await your pleasure."

So she left the room quietly. And when she was gone he walked wildly up and down for a moment. Then he bent and passionately kissed the cushion she had leant on.

Tamara would learn what his love meant, when the day should come.

Chapter Ten

The lunch passed off with quiet reserve, there was no one present but Stephen Strong.

Tamara endeavoured to behave naturally and answered Gritzko whenever he spoke to her. He, too, played his part, but the tone of things did not impose upon Stephen Strong.

As they were leaving the dining-room, on the plea of finding something, Tamara went to her room, and Gritzko took his leave.

"I will fetch you for the French plays to-night, *Tantine*," he said, "and probably will come back to tea, tell Tamara."

So he left, and the two old friends were alone.

They stirred their coffee. There was an awkward silence for a moment, and then the Princess said:

"Stephen, I count upon you to help us all over this. I do not, and will not, even guess what has happened, but of course something has. Only tell me, do you think he loves her? I cannot bear the idea of Tamara's being unhappy."

"If she is prepared never to cross his will, but let him be absolute master of her body and soul, while he makes continuous love to her, I should think she will be the happiest woman in the world.

"She is madly infatuated with him. She has been ever since we came from Egypt, I saw the beginning on the boat, and I warned you, as you know, when I thought he was only fooling."

"In Egypt! They had met before, then!" the Princess exclaimed, surprised. "How like Gritzko to pretend he did not know her, and be introduced all over again!

"They had already quarrelled, I suppose, and that accounts for the cat-and-dog-like tone there has always been between them."

"Probably," said Stephen Strong; "but now I think we can leave it to chance. You may be certain that to marry her is what he wishes most to do, or he would not have asked her."

"Not even if . . . he thought he ought to?"

"No, dear friend. No! I believe I know Gritzko even better than you do. If there was a sense of obligation, and no desire in the case, he would simply shoot her and himself, rather than submit to a fate against his inclination.

"You may rest in peace about that. Whatever strain there is between them, it is not of that sort. I believe he adores her in his odd sort of way; just let them alone now and all will be well."

And greatly comforted, the Princess was able to go out calling.

The news was received with every sort of emotion, surprise, chagrin, joy, excitement, speculation, and there were even those among them who averred they had predicted this marriage all along.

"Fortunately we like her," Countess Olga said. "She is a good sort, and perhaps she will keep Gritzko quiet, and he may be faithful to her."

But this idea was laughed to scorn, until Valonne joined in with his understanding smile.

"I will make you a bet," he said; "in five years' time they will still be love-birds."

Meanwhile Jack Courtray had come in at once to see Tamara.

"Well, upon my word! fancy your marrying a foreigner," he said; "but you have got just about the best chap I have ever met; and I believe you'll be jolly happy."

And Tamara bent down so that he should not see the tears which gathered in her eyes, while she answered softly:

"Thank you very much, Jack; but no one is ever sure of being happy."

And even though Lord Courtray's perceptions were rather thick he wondered at her speech, it upset him.

"Look here, Tamara," he said, "don't you do it then if it is a chancy sort of thing. Don't go and tie yourself up if you aren't sure you love him."

Love him! Good God!

Pent-up feeling overcame Tamara. She answered in a voice her old playmate had never dreamed she possessed, so concentrated and full of passion.

In their English lives they were so accustomed to controlling every feeling into a level commonplace that if they had had time to think, both would have considered this outburst melodramatic.

"Jack," Tamara said, "you don't know what love is. I tell you I know now . . . I love Gritzko so that I would rather be unhappy with him than happy with anyone else on earth.

"And if they ask you at home, say I would not care if he were a Greek, or a Turk. I would follow him to perdition."

She suddenly burst into tears and buried her face in her hands.

Yes, it was true. In spite of shame and disgrace and fear, she loved him, passionately.

Of course Jack, who was the kindest-hearted creature, at once put his arm round her and took out his handkerchief and wiped her eyes, while he said soothingly:

"I say, my child, there! there! this will never do," and he continued to pet and try to comfort her.

But all she could reply was to ask him to go and to promise her not to say anything about her outburst of tears to anyone.

And, horribly distressed, Jack did what she wished, running against Gritzko in the passage as he went out; but they had met before that day, so he did not stop, but, nodding in his friendly way, passed down the stairs.

Tamara sat where he had left her, the tears still trickling over her cheeks, while she stared into the fire. The vision she saw there of her future did not console her.

To be married to a man whom she knew she would daily grow to love more, every moment of her time conscious that the tie was one of suf-

ferance, her pride and self-respect in the dust,
it was a miserable picture.

Gritzko came in so quietly through the ante-
room that, lost in her troubled thoughts, she did
not hear him until he was quite close.

She gave a little startled exclamation and
then looked at him defiantly. She was angry that
he saw her tears.

His face went white and his voice grew
hoarse with overmastering emotion.

"What has happened between you and your
friend, Madame? Tell me the truth. No man
should see you cry! Tell me everything, or I will
kill him."

And he stood there, his eyes blazing.

Then Tamara rose and drew herself to her
full height, while a flash of her vanished pride
returned to her mien, and with great haughtiness
she answered in a cold voice:

"I beg you to understand one thing, Prince,
I will not be insulted by suspicions and threats
against my friends. Lord Courtray and I have
been brought up as brother and sister.

"We spoke of my home, which I may never
see again, and I told him what he was to say to
them there when they asked about me.

"If I have cried I am ashamed of my tears,
and when you speak and act as you have just
done, it makes me ashamed of the feeling which
caused them."

He took a step nearer, he admired her courage.

"What was the feeling which caused them?
Tell me, I must know," he said.

As he spoke he chanced to notice she had replaced her wedding-ring; it shone below his glittering ruby.

"That I will not bear!" he exclaimed.

With almost violence he seized her wrist and forcibly drew both rings from her finger, and then replaced his own.

"There shall be no token of another! No gold band there but mine, and until then, no jewel but this ruby!"

Then he dropped her hand, and turning, threw the wedding-ring with passion in the fire!

Tamara made a step forward in protest, and then she stood petrified while her eyes flashed with anger.

"Indeed, yes, I am ashamed I cried!" she said at last between her teeth.

He made some restless paces, he was very much moved.

"I must know . . ." he began.

But at that moment the servants came in with the tea, and Tamara seized the opportunity to fly from the room, leaving Gritzko extremely disturbed.

What could she mean? He knew in his calmer moments he had not the least cause to be jealous of Jack. What was the inference in her words?

Two weeks seemed a long time to wait before he could have all clouds dispersed, all things explained, as she lay in his arms

And the thought of holding her in his arms drove him wild.

He felt inclined to rush after her, to ask her to forgive him for his anger, to kiss and caress her, to tell her he loved her madly and was jealous of even the air she breathed until he should hear her say she loved him.

He went as far as to write a note.

He determined to keep to the severest formality or he knew he would never be able to play his part until the end.

> Madame:
> I regret my passion just now. The situation seemed peculiar as I came in. I understand there was nothing for me to have been angry about, please forgive me. Rest now. I will come and fetch you at a quarter to eight.
> *Gritzko.*

And as he went away he had it sent to her room.

And when Tamara read it the first gleam of comfort she had known since the night at the hut illumined her thoughts. If he should love her, after all! But no, this could not be so; his behaviour was not that of love.

But in spite of the abiding undercurrent of humiliation and shame, the situation was intensely exciting. She feverishly looked forward to the evening.

Her tears seemed to have unlocked her heart, she was no longer numb. She was perfectly aware that no matter what he had done she loved him wildly.

He had taken everything from her, dragged her down from her pedestal, but she would keep that last remnant of self-respect. He should not know of this crowning humiliation, that she still loved him.

So her manner was like ice when he came into the room, and the chill of it communicated itself to him.

They hardly spoke on the way to the Theatre Michel, and when they entered the box she pretended great interest in the stage, while, between the acts, all their friends came in to give their congratulations.

Tamara asked to be excused from going on to supper and the ball which was taking place. And she kept close to her godmother while going out, and so contrived that she did not say a word alone with Gritzko.

It was because he acquiesced fully in this line of conduct that she was able to carry it through, otherwise he would not have permitted it for a moment.

He realised from this night that the situation could only be made possible if he saw her rarely and before people; alone with her, human nature would be too strong.

So with the most frigid courtesy and ceremony between them the days wore on, and towards the beginning of the following week Gritzko went off with Jack Courtray on the bear-hunt.

He could stand no more.

When he returned there were only five days before the wedding. He had sent her flowers each morning as a lover should, and he had loaded her with presents, all of which she received in the same crushed spirit.

With the fixed idea in her brain that he was only marrying her because as a gentleman he must, none of his gifts gave her any pleasure.

And he, with immense control of passion,

had played his part, only his time of probation
was illumined by the knowledge of coming joy.

Whereas poor Tamara, as the time wore on,
lost all hope, and grew daily paler and more
fragile-looking.

Her father had had a bad attack of the gout,
and could not possibly move; but her brother
Tom and her sister, Lady Newbridge, and Millicent Hardcastle were to arrive three days before
the wedding.

* * *

The night of the bear-hunters' return there
was to be a small dinner at the Ardacheff house.
The Princess had arranged that there should
be a party of six; so that while the four played
bridge the fiancés might talk to one another.

She was growing almost nervous, and indeed
it had required all Stephen Strong's assurance
that things eventually would come right to prevent her from being actually unhappy.

"Let 'em alone!" the old man said. "Take no
notice! You won't regreat it."

Tamara wore a white clinging dress and
seemed a mere slip of a girl.

The great string of beautiful pearls, Gritzko's
latest gift, which had arrived that morning, was
round her neck, and her sweet eyes glanced up
sadly from the blue shadows which encircled
them.

Gritzko was already there when the Princess
and Tamara reached the first Salon, and his eyes
swam with passionate concern when he saw how
Tamara had been suffering.

He could not restrain the feeling in his voice
as he exclaimed:

173

"You have been ill, my sweet lady! Oh!
Tantine, why did you not send for me? How
could you let her suffer?"

And a sudden wave of happiness came over
Tamara when he kissed her hand. She was so
weak the least thing could have made her cry.

But her happiness was short-lived, for
Gritzko, afraid yet of showing what was in his
heart, seemed now colder than ever.

Although he was exulting within himself at
the thought that the moment would come soon
when all this pretence should end.

Tamara, knowing nothing of these things, felt
a new sinking depression. In five days she would
be his wife, and then when he had paid the
honourable price, how would he treat her?

He was looking wildly attractive tonight, his
voice had a thousand tones in it when he addressed the others, he was merry and witty and
gay, and almost made love to the Princess, only
to his fiancée did he seem reserved.

Dinner was an impossible penance, and with
a feverish excitement she waited for the time
when they should be alone.

It seemed an eternity before coffee was finished and the four retired to their bridge. Then
the two passed out of the room and on into the
Blue Salon.

It was extremely difficult for both of them.
The Prince could scarcely control his mad longing to caress her.

Only that strange turn in his character held
him. Also the knowledge that once he were to
grant himself an inch he could never restrain the

whole of his wild passion, and there were yet five days before she should be really his.

Tamara looked a white, frozen shape as she almost fell into the sofa.

Gritzko did not sit beside her. He took a chair and leant on a table near.

"We had good sport," he said dryly. "Your friend can hit things.We got two bears."

"Jack must have been pleased," Tamara answered dully.

"And your family arrive on Monday, don't they?" he asked. "Your brother and sister and the estimable Mrs Hardcastle?"

He laughed as he always did at the mention of Millicent.

"They will wonder, won't they, why you are marrying this savage! But they will not know."

"No!" said Tamara. "They must never know."

Gritzko's face became whimsical, a disconcerting, mischievous provoking smile stole into his eyes.

"Do you know yourself?" he asked.

She looked up at him startled. It was her habit now never to meet his eyes. Indeed, the sense of humiliation under which she lived had changed all her fearless carriage of head.

"Why do you ask such questions? I might as well ask you why you are marrying me. We both know that we cannot help it."

There was a break in her voice which touched him profoundly.

"Answer for yourself, please, I may have several other reasons," he said coldly.

He got up and walked across the room, picking up a bibelot here and there, and replacing it restlessly.

Tamara longed to ask him what these reasons were. She was stirred with a faint hope, but she had not the courage; the intensity of her feeling made her dumb.

"*Tantine* has explained to you the service, I suppose," he said at last. "It is different from yours in your country. It means much more."

"And is more easily broken."

"That is so, but we shall not break ours, except by death," and he raised his head proudly. "From Wednesday onward the rest of your life belongs to me."

Tamara shivered. If she could only overcome this numbness which had returned, if she could only let her frozen heart speak!

This was surely the moment, but she could not, she remained silent and white and lifeless.

He came over to the sofa.

"Tamara," he said, and his voice vibrated with suppressed passion. "Will you tell me the truth. Do hate me, or what do you feel for me?"

She thought he meant only to torture her further; she would not answer the question.

"Is it not enough that you have conquered me by force? Why should you care to know what my feelings are? As you say, after Wednesday I shall belong to you.

"You can strangle me at Milaslav if you wish. My body will be yours, but my soul you shall never soil or touch, you have no part or lot in that matter, Prince."

His eyes filled with pain.

"I will even have your soul," he said.

Then, as though restraining further emotion, he went on coldly:

"I have arranged that after the wedding we go to my house, and do not start for the South until Saturday. There are some things I wish to show you there. Will that be as you wish?"

"I have no wishes, it is as you please," Tamara answered monotonously.

He gave an impatient shrug, and walked up and down the room, his will kept its mastery, but it was a tremendous strain.

Her words had stung him, her intense quiet and absence of emotion had produced a faint doubt. What if after all he should never be able to make her love him?

For the first time in his life a hand of ice clutched his heart. He knew in those moments of agony that she meant the whole world to him.

He glanced at her graceful slender figure so listlessly leaning against the blue cushions, at her pale ethereal face, and then he turned abruptly away towards the door to the other Salon.

"Come," he said, "it is of no avail to talk further, we will say good-night."

Tamara rose. The way to her room led from the opposite side. "Good-night," she said, "make my adieu to Sonia and the rest. I shall go to bed."

She walked away.

The whole floor was between them, as she looked back. He stood rigid by the other door.

Then with great strides he was beside her, and had taken her in his arms.

"Ah! God!" he said, as he fiercely kissed her, then almost flung her from him, and strode from the room.

And Tamara went on to her own, trembling with excitement.

This was passion truly, but what if some love lurked underneath? When she reached her great white bed she fell upon her knees, and burying her face in her hands she prayed to God.

* * *

The wedding was over at last, Gritzko and Tamara were alone. Alone with all their future before them.

Both their faces had been grave and solemn through all the vows and prayers, but afterwards his had shone with a wild triumph. And as they had driven to his house on the Fontonka he held Tamara's hand but had not spoken.

It was a strange eventful moment when he led her up the great stairs between the rows of bowing servants, up into the Salons all decorated with flowers.

Then, still never speaking, he opened the ballroom doors, and when they had walked its great length and came to the rooms beyond, he merely said:

"These you must have done by that man in Paris, or how you please," as if it did not interest him.

Then instead of turning into his own sitting-room, he opened a door on the right, which Tamara did not know, and they entered what had been his mother's bedroom.

It was warmed and lit, but it wore that strange air of gloom and melancholy which untenanted rooms, consecrated to the memory of the dead, always have, in spite of blue satin and bright gilding.

"Tamara," he said, and he took her hand, "these were my mother's rooms. I loved her very much, and I always thought I would never let any woman, not even my wife, enter them. I have left them just as she used them last. But now I know that is not what she would have wished."

His deep voice trembled a little with a note of feeling in it which was new, and which touched Tamara's innermost being.

"I want you to see them now with me, and then while we are in the South all these things shall be taken away, and they shall be left bare and white for you to arrange them when we come back, just as you wish. I want my mother's blessing to rest on us."

Then he paused, and there was a wonderful silence, and when he went on, his tones were full of a great tenderness.

"Little one, in these rooms, someday I will make you happy."

Tamara trembled so she could hardly stand, the reaction from her misery was so immense. She swayed a little and put out her hand to steady herself by the back of a chair.

He thought she was going to fall, seeing her so white, and he put his arm round her as he led her through the room and into the sitting-room, and then beyond again to a little sanctuary.

Here a lamp swung before the Ikon, and the colours were subdued and rich, while the Virgin's soft eyes looked down upon them. There were fresh lilies, too, in a vase below, and their scent perfumed the air.

He knelt for a second and whispered a prayer, then he rose, and they looked into each

179

other's eyes, and their souls met, and all shadows rolled away.

"Tamara!"

He held out his arms, and with a little inarticulate cry almost of pain Tamara fell into them.

He folded her to his heart, while he bent and kissed her hair.

Then he held her from him and looked deep into her eyes.

"Sweetheart, am I forgiven?" he asked.

When she could speak she answered:

"Yes . . . you are forgiven."

Then he questioned again.

"Tamara, do you love me?"

But he saw the answer in her sweet face, and did not wait for her to speak, but kissed her mouth.

Then he lifted her in his arms like a baby and carried her back through the ghostly rooms to his warm human sitting-room, and there he laid her tenderly down upon the couch and knelt beside her.

"Oh, my heart," he said. "What this time has been, since you promised to marry me. But I would not change it, I wanted you to love me beyond everything, beyond anger with me, beyond fear, beyond your pride. Now tell me you do. My sweet one. *Doushka-moia.* I must know. I *must* know. You mean my life. Tell me!"

And passion overcame Tamara, and she answered him in a low voice of vibrating emotion.

"Gritzko! Do you think I care for what you have done or will do! You know very well I have always loved you!"

180

She put up her mouth for him to kiss her.

Then he went quite mad with joy for a few moments. He caressed her as even on the dawn drive she had never dreamed possible.

Presently he said with deep earnestness:

"Darling, we must live for one another, in the world of course for duty; but our real life shall be alone at Milaslav for only you and me. You must teach me to be calm and to banish impossible thoughts.

"You must make yourself my centre, Tamara. You must forget all your former life, and give yourself to me, sweetheart.

"My country must be your country, my body your body, and my soul your soul. I love you better than Heaven or earth, and you are mine now till death do us part."

Then the glory of paradise seemed to descend upon Tamara, as he bent and kissed her lips.

Oh! what did anything else matter in the world since after all he loved her! This beautiful fierce lover!

Visions of enchantment presented themselves, a complete intoxication of joy.

He held her in his arms, and all the strange passion and mystic depths which had fascinated her always, now dwelt in his eyes, only intensified by delirious love.

"Do you remember, sweetheart, how you defied and resisted me? Darling! Heart of mine! but I have conquered you and taken you, in spite of all! You cannot struggle any more, you are my own.

"Only you must tell me that you give me,

too, your soul. You said once I should have no part
or lot in your soul. But, Tamara, tell me that I
have it?"

And Tamara thrilled with ecstasy as she
whispered:

"Yes, you have it."

She cared not at all about pride, she did not
wish to struggle; she adored being conquered.
Her entire being was merged in his.

He held her from him for a second and the
old whimsical smile full of tender mischief stole
into his eyes.

"That night at the hut, when you dropped
the pistol—don't you want to know what really
did happen?" he asked.

She buried her face in his scarlet coat.

"Oh, no, no, no!" she cried. "It is all forgotten and forgiven."

Then with wild passion he clasped her to his
breast as he cried:

"Oh! Love! My sweet Princess; the gods are
very kind to us, for all happiness is yet to come.
I did but kiss your little feet."

ABOUT THE EDITOR

BARBARA CARTLAND, the celebrated romantic author, historian, playwright, lecturer, political speaker and television personality, has now written over 150 books. Miss Cartland has had a number of historical books published and several biographical ones, including that of her brother, Major Ronald Cartland, who was the first Member of Parliament to be killed in the War. This book had a Foreword by Sir Winston Churchill.

In private life, Barbara Cartland, who is a Dame of the Order of St. John of Jerusalem, has fought for better conditions and salaries for Midwives and nurses. As President of the Royal College of Midwives (Hertfordshire Branch), she has been invested with the first Badge of Office ever given in Great Britain, which was subscribed to by the Midwives themselves. She has also championed the cause for old people and founded the first Romany Gypsy Camp in the world.

Barbara Cartland is deeply interested in Vitamin Therapy and is President of the British National Association for Health.

Barbara Cartland

The world's bestselling author of romantic fiction. Her stories are always captivating tales of intrigue, adventure and love.

☐	THE TEARS OF LOVE	2148	$1.25
☐	THE DEVIL IN LOVE	2149	$1.25
☐	THE ELUSIVE EARL	2436	$1.25
☐	THE BORED BRIDEGROOM	6381	$1.25
☐	JOURNEY TO PARADISE	6383	$1.25
☐	THE PENNILESS PEER	6387	$1.25
☐	NO DARKNESS FOR LOVE	6427	$1.25
☐	THE LITTLE ADVENTURE	6428	$1.25
☐	LESSONS IN LOVE	6431	$1.25
☐	THE DARING DECEPTION	6435	$1.25
☐	CASTLE OF FEAR	8103	$1.25
☐	THE GLITTERING LIGHTS	8104	$1.25
☐	A SWORD TO THE HEART	8105	$1.25
☐	THE MAGNIFICENT MARRIAGE	8166	$1.25
☐	THE RUTHLESS RAKE	8240	$1.25
☐	THE DANGEROUS DANDY	8280	$1.25
☐	THE WICKED MARQUIS	8467	$1.25
☐	LOVE IS INNOCENT	8505	$1.25
☐	THE FRIGHTENED BRIDE	8780	$1.25
☐	THE FLAME IS LOVE	8887	$1.25

Barbara Cartland

The world's bestselling author of romantic fiction. Her stories are always captivating tales of intrigue, adventure and love.

☐	THE CRUEL COUNT	2128	$1.25
☐	CALL OF THE HEART	2140	$1.25
☐	AS EAGLES FLY	2147	$1.25
☐	THE MASK OF LOVE	2366	$1.25
☐	AN ARROW OF LOVE	2426	$1.25
☐	A GAMBLE WITH HEARTS	2430	$1.25
☐	A KISS FOR THE KING	2433	$1.25
☐	A FRAME OF DREAMS	2434	$1.25
☐	THE FRAGRANT FLOWER	2435	$1.25
☐	MOON OVER EDEN	2437	$1.25
☐	THE GOLDEN ILLUSION	2449	$1.25
☐	FIRE ON THE SNOW	2450	$1.25
☐	THE HUSBAND HUNTERS	2461	$1.25
☐	THE SHADOW OF SIN	0430	$1.25
☐	SAY YES, SAMANTHA	7834	$1.25
☐	THE KARMA OF LOVE	8106	$1.25
☐	BEWITCHED	8630	$1.25
☐	THE IMPETUOUS DUCHESS	8705	$1.25

Bantam Book Catalog

It lists over a thousand money-saving bestsellers originally priced from $3.75 to $15.00 —bestsellers that are yours now for as little as 60¢ to $2.95!

The catalog gives you a great opportunity to build your own private library at huge savings!

So don't delay any longer—send us your name and address and 25¢ (to help defray postage and handling costs).